FIRE
A Cal Jamison Mystery

by Linda Kuhlmann

This novel is fictional. The names, characters, events and places in this novel are products of the author's imagination or are used fictitiously. Any similarity to real persons, living or dead, is coincidental and not intended by the author.

ISBN: 978-0-9858333-4-3
ISBN-13: 978-0-9858333-4-3

Cover Design by Fireside Design Studio
Images used under license from Shutterstock.com

Other Books by
Linda Kuhlmann

The Red Boots

Koenig Triple Crown series
Koenig's Wonder
Koenig's Spirit
Koenig's Promise

ACKNOWLEDGMENTS

In writing this fascinating story, I received assistance from so many people that it is impossible to name them all. To everyone, I express my deepest thanks.

In addition, I would like to express my gratitude to the following people for their expertise, help, and encouragement. Although the final responsibility for the accuracy of the text is mine, I could not have completed this novel without these special people: Dr. Jana Van Amberg; Colonel Eric Thompson; Kai Aspelin; Elmer Carr; Dan Homeres; Jeff Perin; Jeff Clay; Jason James; Dr. Gary Boehne; Riley Sanders; Carrie Patten; Judie Braaten and Karla Fry.

Finally, a special thank you to my husband for his infinite patience and support.

PROLOGUE

LUTHER GREEVES COULD SEE the blaze coming out of the plastics manufacturing building as their Deschutes County fire truck approached. Two engines were already on site with men working to put water on the flames. Luther was the captain of the Search & Rescue Squad, which meant they were the first to go into a burning building to see if anyone was still inside. He'd been volunteering for the fire department now for over eight years – ever since he got out of the Army.

Visions of the blazes he'd caused while in his military duty flashed through his mind, but he thrust them back into the depths where he kept them hidden. It was only moments like this that they'd resurface and he didn't have time for that now.

As Luther parked their vehicle, he looked at his team. Two crew members always worked together inside a fire scene. Karen Burke was ex-military and had been with him now for two years. Jeremy Lockhart was a young volunteer who'd shown great proficiency at the Fire Academy when

Luther had a spot to fill. Jeremy was also the son of the county's fire chief.

"Okay," Luther said as he started toward the back of the vehicle, fastening his turnout coat. "I'm first going in." He grabbed his helmet and gloves and was about to assign Karen to join him when Jeremy stopped him.

"Captain," the young redhead said, "I want to go in with you, okay?"

Luther looked up at the flames and black smoke roiling out of the two-story building windows. "Not this time."

He saw the look on Jeremy's face. Luther turned to Karen. When she nodded, he said to the young man, "Alright, you can be my second…"

He knew Karen usually had his back when entering a building, but she understood that Jeremy needed the experience. The rule was one firefighter was always left outside to assist as needed.

He and Jeremy put on their Scott air masks and helmets. Then, Luther checked his microphone.

"OK, can everyone hear me?"

When the others nodded, he said, "You know the drill. We'll keep radio contact so Karen knows what's going on inside."

The woman saluted and smiled. "I've got this, sir."

"Karen, you don't have to salute me," he said, smiling. He kind of liked being called 'sir.'

She nodded. "You're coming through loud and clear."

"Ready, Jeremy?"

"Roger that." The young man adjusted the fire axe on his belt.

Taking a deep breath and saying a silent prayer as he always did, Luther walked up to the building. He paused a moment and thought of his wife, Jamie, and their two kids. Then, standing to one side, he forcibly opened the door with his Halligan, a tool used by firefighters and police to forcibly enter a building. Waiting a moment to avoid any backdraft, he walked into the burning structure, knowing this could be his last one.

The heat forced him back a step and even after a few minutes, he started perspiring profusely inside his Nomex turnout gear. The smoke was a thick, black cloud, so dense he had to lean down to see.

He turned to make sure Jeremy was still following him. As they walked past a forklift on their left, Luther thought he saw something on the propane tank, but then his attention was turned to flames coming from a mezzanine hanging overhead. It was only supported on one side. He was about to report to Karen when he saw a brilliant flash. The explosion forced both men to hit the ground and flames cut through the smoke overhead.

"Captain, you okay?" Luther heard Karen say in his microphone.

"Yes, but Jeremy…"

He rushed to the young man who was clawing at his face – his helmet and air mask had blown away in the explosion and he couldn't breathe.

"Firefighter down!" Luther yelled. "We're on the east side - in about fifty feet."

Knowing it was against all rules, Luther took off one glove, removed his helmet so he could place his air mask on Jeremy's face, trying to calm the panicked young firefighter.

As he quickly took a couple of breaths of compressed air himself, Luther looked up and saw that the mezzanine was now totally engulfed in flames. Suddenly, it crashed down over them…

JAMIE GREEVES RAN INTO the hospital and frantically asked the reception clerk which room her husband was in. When she arrived, Fire Chief Gordon Lockhart was there. He was a burly man with red hair and was wearing his uniform.

"I'm so sorry, Jamie..." the captain began, placing an arm around her shoulders. He'd known Luther for ten years – even before he'd started volunteering at the fire department. He fought back tears as he said, "We lost Jeremy..."

"Oh, Gordon," Jamie said, hugging the older man. "Jeremy was your only child."

When she saw Luther lying there with his head, face and one hand bandaged, her heart sank, even though she was secretly relieved he was still alive. He was hooked up with a tube for oxygen.

"Luther, honey," Jamie said as she walked up to her husband. She took his left hand and kissed it gently, rubbing her thumb over his wedding band.

When he didn't respond, she softly said his name again. She could see his eyes moving rapidly behind his eyelids as if he was reliving a nightmare. Then, he opened them with a start and frantically glanced around the room as if he was somewhere else. He stared at her.

"Luther..." she said softly.

The doctor entered and checked his chart, but Luther just continued to stare at the woman next to him.

"Who are you?" His voice was raspy and he coughed for a few seconds.

"He's lucky to be alive, Mrs. Greeves," the doctor said. "Besides the burns and other injuries from the fire, I'm afraid he may possibly be suffering from post-traumatic amnesia. Depending on the extent of damage to his brain, it could be temporary...but it may also be permanent."

IN A HOTEL ROOM across town, a man sat at a table, drinking a beer and feeling pleased with himself. He ran his fingers through his dark hair and replayed his steps in his mind of when he had entered that plastics building. He'd been in the building before and knew exactly what he needed to do.

First thing was to place the C4 pack that was connected to a remote burner phone near the valve of the propane tank on a forklift sitting midway from the entrance. He'd learned a lot about explosives in the military.

When he'd secured the device with a magnet, he looked up at the mezzanine where the offices were. Climbing the steps, he visualized how it all would play out. The small space heater near one of the desks was perfect for what he planned. He opened opposite windows to create a draft. Then, he spread papers all over the area to create a fire trail throughout the office. Spying a large overcoat hanging nearby, he'd put it where the heater sat. Taking out a small bottle from his pocket, he sprayed some Isopropyl alcohol on an outlet, the material and the papers nearby, and then he plugged in and turned on the heater. Laying the coat over that, he'd stepped back and watched as it all caught flame.

He knew how much time he needed to get out of the building. Then, he'd waited outside a ways back in some trees until the billows of black smoke and red flames appeared from the open windows. He watched awhile longer, pleased with himself. Finally, he called 911 from another burner phone to anonymously report the fire.

The long minutes it took for the fire trucks to arrive had seemed like hours. But, still he waited for the Search and Rescue truck to drive up. When the firefighters dismounted, he nodded, seeing the man he wanted. He then dialed all the numbers on the other phone - except one. He'd held the cell phone in his hand and waited for the right moment...

He'd felt justified when the explosion went off, yelling, *Die*!

Now, as he watched the evening's news about the fire on the television, he jumped to his feet when he saw a woman firefighter being interviewed. In the background, Luther Greeves was alive, lying on a gurney as he was being wheeled towards an ambulance.

"Damn!" the man yelled, throwing the beer bottle against the wall. As the glass shattered, he realized his plan had failed.

Slowly, he sat down and started to plot the next time he would get the chance to kill his nemesis.

CHAPTER 1

One Year Later

CAL JAMISON STEPPED OUT of the steaming shower. He needed the heat to warm his muscles at the beginning of every day now. As he dried off, the towel rubbed against the ugly red scar that ran from his right clavicle, over his shoulder and six inches down his back – a constant reminder of the explosion that almost ended his career as a Marine. Visions of that event stopped him cold every time he allowed himself to remember the three men he'd lost on that mission.

He'd been in the Marines now for twenty years and did numerous missions in the Middle East and all over the world – until that fateful blast the previous year in Afghanistan. His therapy was almost over now and he was about to re-up. Camp Lejeune seemed a million miles away.

Cal wiped the steam from the mirror with his hand, his dark hair and eyes reflected back at him. He liked that he had his grandmother's Northern Paiute coloring, which made him stand out among the other boys in his family. His three brothers and mother still lived on the massive

Jamison Ranch near the Crooked River, north of Terrebonne.

Walking into his new bedroom at his grandfather's ranch, Cal was grateful for Glenn giving him a place to stay while on medical leave. He knew how obsessive his mother would be with caring for him and he didn't need that right now.

His grandparents insisted everyone call them by their given names and Cal never asked why. But, he understood the need to pull away from the large Jamison homestead. Glenn had done the same thing years ago and named his smaller ranch after James Jamison, their ancestor who immigrated with his family to New York in 1802.

IT WAS STILL PRE-DAWN when Cal carried his boots and tiptoed out of the log home that Glenn built in 1992 – the same year Cal joined the military. The Double J Ranch was located near Tumalo, Oregon. It was Glenn's little slice of heaven, with twenty head of cattle and a small herd of adopted Kiger horses.

Cal loved the feel of the cool morning air on his face and took a deep breath of the sharp odor of Ponderosa Pine trees. It was good to be home. He put on his boots and smiled as he was greeted by Glenn's Australian Shepherd.

"Hey, Odie," he said as the dog wriggled his entire body, happy to see someone. His black and copper coat shone in the early light.

Cal scratched the white chest of the dog, then walked to his '58 Jeep Wrangler that Glenn bought for him when he'd learned to drive. The October sun was now just coming up over the horizon, so he removed the CJ7's soft top, zipped up his vest and got in. A black-billed Magpie flew overhead, its long, iridescent-green tail and wings shone as it squawked on its way.

As Cal pulled out, he looked at the horizon where his Cessna Skyhawk stood in the open hangar at the end of the grassy runway. That was his dad's first airplane that Cal inherited simply because he was the only pilot in his family at the time. He shook his head and drove on, still hoping that someday he'd get his revenge for his father's death.

Cal thought of Callum Jamison, his namesake. Callum came to America with his parents from Scotland, then, at age nineteen, he went west on his own to work in the fur trading business. In the 1820s, Callum left the Ogden party, built a homestead in the Crooked River Valley and called it the Jamison Ranch. Cal was a seventh-generation Jamison to live in Oregon and was proud of his heritage – just not what his brother, Jack, was doing with the land their ancestors had settled.

Shaking off the memories, Cal turned onto Route 97 and smiled as he saw the snowy tops of the Three Sisters luminous in the early sun, a mountain range he'd come to love. Mt. Bachelor stood in the distance to the south. He pulled his fleece vest collar up around his neck in the cool air. Fall was his favorite time of year.

The traffic was a steady stream of cars now as he approached Bend. Cal was meeting his best friend, Micco, for breakfast. This had become a ritual ever since Cal's brother started acting like king of the castle on the Jamison, even though his mother was the actual land owner. The feud with Cal's brother went back seventeen years – just after their father was shot and killed.

CHAPTER 2

CAL DROVE INTO DOWNTOWN Bend and found a parking space on Bond Street. As he entered the D&D Bar and Grill, the oldest bar in town, he saw the Christmas lights hanging over the bar that the owner left up all year long. A recap of the previous night's World Series game was on all of the TV screens around the room. He smiled when he read the familiar sign over the cash register that said: *Unattended children will be given espresso and a free kitten.*

A song by a fairly new Country singer, Easton Corbin, was playing on the juke box. The steamy place was fairly empty except for a few locals.

The D&D was also a hangout for the local firefighters. He looked for Luther Greeves among the group of men sitting at one table, but he wasn't there. Luther had survived a major arson fire the previous year, but his friend still hadn't fully regained his memory of that event.

Micco, a Northern Paiute like Cal's grandmother, was already at the bar, nursing a hangover with a Screwdriver. He was a small man, yet strong and lithe. He was Cal's best friend and they were both born on the Jamison. Micco's father was the large ranch's foreman.

"Hey, buddy," Cal said as he sat down next to his friend, slapping him on the back.

"Keep it down, man," Micco said, wincing, holding his head.

A petite Asian woman with long black hair came over and set a Bloody Mary in front of Cal. "I made it just the way you like it, with only one olive."

"Thanks, Hana," he said and winked at her as he ate the olive.

Hana was Cal's biology partner in high school. Her mother was originally from South Korea - came to the U.S. after the Korean War with Hana's father, an Army soldier. When Hana started working at the D&D, she tried to bring a few Korean dishes into the menu, but Barney, the owner, didn't like it.

Cal ordered his usual breakfast of steak and eggs. Micco asked for biscuits and gravy.

Hana leaned over the counter in front of Micco and smiled. "Do you want hot sauce with that?"

"Sure," was all Micco said, but Cal knew his friend was doomed.

Cal watched as the small woman single-handedly worked both the bar and restaurant orders and still kept smiling. The place was beginning to fill up.

"She's got the hots for you, my friend," Cal told Micco.

"Speaking of hot chicks, how did your date go with that cute blonde last Friday?"

Cal took a few gulps of his Bloody Mary, then said, "It was okay. We went to the movies."

"What'd you see?"

"A chick flick." Cal groaned. "I pretty much listened to the noise of the action film in the next cinema, wishing I was there."

"You going to ask her out again?"

"Probably not."

"You seem to never get past the first date anymore. How come?"

Cal looked down the bar at a couple of loggers who had just entered before answering. "You know the reason."

Micco grunted, then said, "Why aren't you in worse shape? We pounded a lot of booze last night."

"Training," Cal said with a smile. "You can't go on missions like I do with a hangover."

"I used to be able to drink you under the table."

"Not anymore. How's the 'King' today?" Cal asked about his brother, Jack.

Micco laughed. "He's still sitting on his throne." He took a drink, wiped his mouth with the back of his hand and added, "But, he wants you to come back to the kingdom."

Cal shook his head. "Not in this lifetime!"

He rolled his right shoulder to ease the dull pain, which he knew his friend had seen. Micco retired from the military the previous March, when his mother died. His job was in a Marine Communications Unit. Unlike Cal, Micco had never been in any combat, but from some of the reports he'd read, he understood what his buddy must have gone through.

"Your hair's growing back," Cal said, laughing. "Remember the fit your dad threw when we came home on leave after Basic Training?"

Micco ran his hand over the new stubble. "Yeah. Being a Northern Paiute, I never cut my hair before that."

Cal took a sip of his drink and said, "We were just kids then."

"Eighteen and determined."

"Yep," Cal said. "I couldn't get away from the Jamison fast enough."

Micco looked at his friend. "When you going back to your base?"

Cal shrugged his shoulders, but he tried not to grimace. "In two weeks, I guess."

After Hana brought their food and left, Micco asked, "How's Glenn doing?"

Cal had been surprised to see the change in his grandfather when he returned. "He may need more help now on the Double J – even though he won't admit it."

He cut some steak, but didn't eat. Putting down his fork, Cal looked at his friend. "I'm worried about him. He has always been larger than life, smoking his pipe as he worked the cattle or dancing a jig in his kilt with Grandma Winnie."

The two silently dug into their food. After a few moments, Cal looked at Micco in the mirror behind the bar and said, "What the hell would I do if something happens to him? Being a Marine is all I know."

Micco smiled. "You'd think of something."

CHAPTER 3

OUTSIDE, TWO WOMEN WERE walking toward the D&D – a petite blonde and a tall brunette. Just before they crossed the street, two small convertibles passed them and parked in the nearby bank lot. One was a silver and black color, the other, a fire engine red.

"Wow," the blonde woman said to one of the drivers. "What kind of cars are those?"

A tall, silver-haired man in the red car said, "They're Morgans – built in England. My wife and I have had it for ten years." His wife with fiery red hair smiled and got out.

The women walked over to get a closer look at the sporty cars with the bug-eyed headlights and long, swooping fenders.

One of the men said, "Morgans have been manufactured in Malvern since 1909 and are still being made there today. They have a wood frame."

"You're joking?" the brunette said.

"I love it when we go over railroad tracks," the redhead said smiling. "The entire car shifts under your butt."

"Ours is a 1958 Plus Four," her husband added.

"What does that mean?" the blonde asked.

As he put a leather cover over the seats, he explained. "The first Morgans were three-wheelers. This model has four wheels and bigger cylinders. It's a two-seater roadster that has a long hood and wire wheels and resembles vintage 1930s cars with a spare tire on the back." He looked around and asked, "We hear there's a good breakfast place near here."

"The D&D, just across the street," the blonde said, pointing to the building with the red neon sign above the door. "We'll see you in there."

The two women left.

AS THEY ENTERED THE local haunt, the blonde saw the two men at the bar and said, "Well, look at what the cat drug in."

"Hi, Jamie," Cal said as he stood and hugged Luther Greeves' wife. Micco only waved and went back to his food.

Cal glanced at the striking brunette in colorful clothes standing next to Jamie. He put out a hand and said, "We haven't met. I'm Cal Jamison."

The brunette took his hand in hers. "I'm Mary Creswell, Jamie's sister from Seattle."

"Well, it's nice to meet you, Mary." Cal turned and introduced Micco. Then, he looked back at the door and asked, "Where's your ugly husband, Jamie?"

"Oh, Luther's off hunting again. He got his Elk Tag and insisted on going alone." Jamie looked away a moment, then turned back and said, "He does that sometimes when something's bothering him."

Cal decided to not ask. He'd been in Pakistan when

he'd heard about Luther's narrow escape with death in that fire. After he got home, Micco told Cal about Luther's memory loss…and how a few things were starting to come back.

Jamie chatted about the strangers they'd met outside and their cool cars. Then she said, "Come on, Mary, I'm starving."

The women sat in a booth across the room.

"That sister of Jamie's is a looker," Micco said as he finished his meal.

"Hm-mm," was all Cal said. He turned and looked again at the woman in the teal, orange, and red Paisley jacket. He'd never seen colors like that mixed together – except maybe on his grandmother.

"I'm thinking about going fishing this afternoon, after I get some chores finished at the Double J," Cal said. "Want to come?"

"Nah," Micco said as he took the last sip of his drink. "Dad's got some fences for me to mend at the big ranch."

A commotion at the door made all the locals look up. Four people, who must have been Jamie's tourists she'd talked about, entered and found a couple of tables in the middle of the room. The men immediately sat down, while the ladies rearranged some chairs, swapping out wobbly ones for a better seat.

Once all were settled, Jamie leaned over across the aisle, smiled and said to the redhead, "That's not how we play musical chairs around here."

Cal and Micco were ready to leave, so Cal walked over toward Jamie's booth to say goodbye. He overheard one of the tourists talking to his friend about the 'Morgan Wobble.' Cal leaned over and said, "You're lucky, sir. My Jeep Wrangler has what's known as a 'Death Wobble'."

Just then, Cal's cell phone rang. He answered it and heard his grandmother's worried voice say, "Glenn's been taken to the hospital!"

CHAPTER 4

THE SIGHT OF CAL'S grandmother alone in the hospital's waiting room was like a knife in his chest. Winnie Jamison was a small woman with a weathered face and dark brown eyes. She sat wringing a white handkerchief in her hands, a nervous habit she'd had since a child. He went up and hugged her.

"How is he?" he asked softly. Micco stood silently nearby.

She rose from her chair and looked up at Cal with tears in her eyes. Shaking her head, she said, "I don't know. They won't let me see him yet."

Cal saw the anger flash in Micco's eyes, knowing their family's history. "What happened?" he asked.

"He went out to check the horses," Winnie began. "Odie came barking at the house and would not quiet until I followed him to the stable. I found Glenn collapsed in the aisle." She wiped her eyes and continued, "I called for an ambulance, but that waiting...until they could arrive..." She sat as she took a deep breath. "I thought I'd lost him."

"I'll get some coffee," Micco said, leaving the two alone.

Cal sat next to his grandmother and took her small hand in his. He wasn't sure what he'd do if Glenn was no longer in his life. When Cal was fifteen, his own father was killed. Glenn had stepped in and helped him become the man he was today.

"I'm sure he'll be back on his feet, dancing a Ceilidh with you..." he said to try to get his grandmother to smile. The Ceilidh was a traditional Scottish dance that Glenn taught Winnie when they'd first met. "Either that or he'll break into a Highland Fling."

Winnie did smile a little. "Yes, one night we were dancing, I sprained my ankle and we had to go to the hospital—" She suddenly stopped.

"It'll be okay," he said. "I'm here now."

"I'm so grateful for you, dear one," she said as she patted his cheek.

Cal jumped to his feet when Henry Blake came through the double doors. Henry had been the Jamison family doctor since he arrived in Bend from Portland over sixty years ago.

"Winnie, Cal," Dr. Blake said and sat down next to Winnie. "Glenn is resting now. He had another mild stroke."

"Oh, no," Cal's grandmother sighed.

"He will need three to six months recovery, but we all know how stubborn he is. I tried to explain that to him, but he's insisting to check himself out – against my advice."

"Yes," Cal said, "we understand. But, this time I'm here. Can we see him now?"

"Yes, follow me."

WHEN THEY REACHED GLENN'S room, the large man was sitting up. His fading red hair was disheveled and his face was more ashen than usual. Yet, he was scratching his beard, asking the nurse if he could have his pipe back.

"You know you can't smoke in here, Mr. Jamison," the nurse said.

When Glenn saw his family enter, he smiled. "Ah, here's the bonnie love of my life."

Winnie hugged him. "You scared me to death!"

He kissed his wife. "I'm sorry, sweat pea. Didn't know that was going to happen."

Just then, Micco entered with cups of coffee.

Glenn took one and looked at the doctor. "So, Henry, when can I get out of here? I've got work to do."

"I still have more tests. This is your second stroke in two years and there's a chance you could have another – or worse. You will need to make some changes, like no red meat—"

"You know that I raise cattle for a living!"

"No matter, we need to get your blood pressure and cholesterol under control." Henry took the coffee cup from Glenn and added,. "And, no caffeine."

Cal caught Glenn's glance and saw something in his eyes he'd never seen before, which frightened him. "I wish I didn't have to go back to active duty soon," he said.

When Micco heard this, he stepped in. "Mr. Jamison, I could come help. Then you can recoup at home."

"Call me Glenn," the older man told Micco. "Are you sure your dad can do without you at the Jamison Ranch?"

Micco smiled. "He has other hands – I'm sure he'll manage."

"I'd appreciate that," Glenn said to thank the young man.

Cal was glad to see his grandfather agree to Micco's offer. He looked at Winnie standing next to Glenn, seeing the fear in her eyes. She didn't trust medical doctors, but had learned to accept Glenn's ways about some things. At that moment, Cal knew he had a big decision to make.

"Okay, Henry," Glenn said, scratching his aging red beard. "I'll give you a couple more days in here on one condition."

"What's that?" the doctor asked.

Glenn looked at Cal and smiled. "That my grandson keeps the rest of the Jamisons away. I don't want a lot of fussing while I'm stuck in here."

"Understood," Cal said.

Glenn winked at his wife and squeezed her hand. "I'm not dying in this place, that's for damned sure – I just want to get home."

CHAPTER 5

LUTHER GREEVES SAT OUTSIDE his tent in what was known as the China Hat area south of Brothers. This was his favorite hunting spot for big game. It was remote and hidden from view because of the rocky ledges nearby.

He sipped Jack Daniels as he reminisced that he'd been hunting since he was twelve years old. His dad taught him to hunt rabbits and squirrels in the woods near Klamath Falls, then moved him on to deer. Luther's dad, Larry Greeves, was an abusive drunk and they hadn't spoken since Luther left when he was seventeen. Now, any time Luther thought of his father, his anger would resurface. He threw another log on the fire and watched the sparks drift skyward.

As he took another long shot of whiskey, Luther saw his hand shake and knew his PTSD was kicking in again. His military experience didn't start until after he and Jamie were married. Their son, Riley, was born, but then Jamie miscarried a few times after that. Frustrated and feeling like a failure, Luther joined the Army to help support his family. He was on Active Duty for four years, then in the Reserves. He'd liked his basic training and then his special training at Fort Sill, Oklahoma to become a Forward Observer. A shudder ran through him as he remembered the consequences of some of those missions.

His daughter, Josie, was born the year he'd returned.

A horse whinnied and Luther walked over where Champ was tethered to a picket line. The gelding was a gentle white and black piebald Gypsy Cob that he'd bought shortly after he and Jamie got married. He rode Champ during the various rodeo parades he'd participated in, where he was a bull riding star.

"What's the matter, old boy," he said to the horse as he stroked the spotted neck. "You lonely?"

Champ nickered in response and leaned his head against Luther's chest. They stood like that for some time, then he checked Champ's feed and water and said good night.

As he walked back to the campfire, he was glad for this week to himself. He'd been working at Holt Construction for two months now, even if it was only for a few hours a week. He needed to ease into the job again since he still wasn't himself yet. There were things he couldn't remember that bugged him, and there was something he knew he had to do.

After the fire last year, it took him months to even remember who his wife and kids were. That incident had scrambled his brains and caused more damage to his lungs than he let on. He'd tried to help Jeremy, the young fireman caught in that fire with him. Luther knew how stupid he'd been taking off his own helmet and mask, to give him oxygen. But, the young man didn't survive.

Luther went into his tent and picked up his backpack. Sitting down on his cot, he pulled out some papers and started leafing through them. He noted Jerry Holt's name as the owner of Hawk's Plastics building.

He looked up at the lantern burning overhead. Luther could only recall a few images, but they were still foggy. The main reason Luther started working at his new job was to see if he could learn something about Holt. He didn't trust the man.

When he came across the fire investigator's report, he stopped. A few days ago, Luther found a way to get into the department's office and get this file. He needed to see what Seth Richards had written about the incident at Hawk's Plastics. Seth's recap looked thorough, like many others Luther had seen after the numerous fires he'd served on.

He skimmed down the page to Seth's cause of the blaze: *Faulty wiring originating in the mezzanine level offices.* But, that determination just didn't fit with Luther's recollections now. He did remember the explosion that took down Jeremy. Reading further down, Seth had concluded that a forklift propane tank had been the source for that. Then, shortly after, the mezzanine had fallen down on them.

"I know there's something I'm missing," Luther said to himself in frustration. If only he could remember…

CHAPTER 6

A COUPLE OF DAYS later, Cal flew his Skyhawk to the Jamison, the large family ranch in the Crooked River Valley. He wasn't looking forward to seeing some of his family, knowing that every time they were together, there would be an argument. Glenn was home now at the Double J and Micco was moving there today.

Cal banked the small Cessna northeast toward Redmond, a central Oregon town in the High Desert, named after pioneer settlers in the early 1900s. He'd heard the stories of how the Redmond family had to take weekly water trips to Cline Falls until the irrigation canal reached their farm.

As he continued north near Terrebonne, the colorful Smith Rock came into view. Cal loved climbing and hiking there, even in winter when the temperatures could get below freezing. Iron caused the hardened lava rock to turn almost red in the sunlight. He circled over and looked down at the Crooked River that had carved its way through this incredible part of the earth's beautiful history.

In a few minutes, he was flying over Jamison land. It reached thousands of acres, but he smiled when he saw the saw mill and log buildings of the old homestead that Callum Jamison started over a hundred years ago. Every time he came here, Cal couldn't resist this area of the ranch, which had been abandoned in 1910, after Fergus Jamison, Glenn's grandfather, built the newer home. Fergus also built the saw mill around that time. These were reminders Cal loved of his family's heritage.

Eventually, he landed his plane on the ranch's airstrip and parked it next to the Cessna 185 Skywagon. He'd helped select that larger plane when they needed an aircraft to locate cattle and carry feed to the remote ranges. He made sure that plane had been fitted with over-sized, low-pressure Tundra tires because of the rough range landings.

He smiled when his younger brother, Tate, came walking out of the hangar, wiping his hands on a shop rag. He was four years younger and had their dad's sandy hair and blue eyes. Cal taught him to fly before he left for the military. Later, Tate trained as an airplane mechanic and sometimes worked at the Redmond airport just to get away from the family dynamics.

Cal grabbed an empty box from the back and stepped out of the plane.

"Hey, Cal," Tate said, "what're you doing here?"

"I came to get the rest of my stuff and help Micco pack."

Tate's eyes looked toward the large log house, where the rest of Cal's family still lived. Then the young man said, "I figured you'd do that someday, but was hoping I was wrong." After a bit, Tate asked, "How's granddad doing?"

"He's home. I'm sure he'd like it if you stopped by the Double J sometime to see him. But, don't mention it to anyone else for now."

Cal looked toward the house and barn. "Where's Ma?" he asked.

"She and Jack went to Portland for a corporate meeting. Clyde's gone into Prineville for a load of hay…"

Cal was glad he wouldn't see his mother, but sad his other brother, Clyde, wasn't there – he was the peacemaker in the family, named after their great-great grandfather. Cal was hoping to get in and out as fast as he could.

HE WALKED TO THE long one-story house made of Lodgepole Pine logs and entered the high-ceilinged foyer and living room. A chandelier made of deer antlers hung overhead, which Cal never liked.

The familiar smell of pine and varnish struck him as he entered the great room. It was still warm from an earlier fire that smolder behind a screen in the large volcanic rock fireplace, like the one at the historic Great Hall in Sunriver. His eyes immediately went to his dad's rifle, still hanging over the mantel.

In the hallway toward his old bedroom hung old black and white pictures of his ancestors who had lived there. He paused at each image in respect of the strength and resilience it must have taken to survive in those times.

One photo was taken when the house was under construction. He marveled at the ingenuity of the men, wearing suit vests and hats, as they guided the large logs to their resting place on one outside wall. The women in long black skirts, white blouses and hats watched nearby.

Continuing down the long hall, he turned into his old bedroom. Standing in one corner was his acoustic guitar he hadn't played in years. On the tall dresser sat a black cap with 'CJ' embroidered in white thread that he wore in high school, the brim still perfectly shaped. Growing up on the Jamison Ranch had its good times and bad.

Cal quickly began to pack.

AS HE WALKED OUT of the big house, carrying the last of his things, Cal found Micco packing a wooden crate with computer equipment into his Dodge Ram pickup. His Paint horse was already in the trailer.

"I'm done here," Cal said. "How about you?"

"That's my last load." Micco attached the Tonneau cover on the back to keep his equipment secure. He looked at the guitar case and smiled. "Hope this means you're going to start playing again."

Wes, Micco's dad, rode up to the barn on a black stallion. He dismounted and came over to where Cal and Micco stood. He was not a tall man, slightly bent over from years of labor. His long hair was gray at the roots, but he was still strong. Wes was Winnie's second cousin.

"How's your granddad doing, Cal?" the older man asked.

"Glad he's home."

"Oh, I bet," Wes said smiling. "That old coot never did like hospitals."

Seeing Cal looking around nervously, Micco said, "Well, Dad, I'm ready to roll."

"Well, I'd better be going," Cal said. He turned to the older man and said, "It was nice seeing you again, Wes." Then, he walked toward his plane.

Wes looked at Micco. "Watch out for Cal, son."

"That's my plan." He hugged his dad, got into his truck and drove off.

AT THE HANGAR, TATE said, "I've refueled for you."

Cal's brother was leaning against the fuselage with his arms crossed. By his body language, Cal could tell Tate didn't like what he was doing. But, by now, Cal had no choice.

Tate watched as his brother stowed the box and guitar case in the cargo compartment. These two brothers had always been tighter than the rest, simply because they were the closest to their dad.

"Please don't go," Tate begged, placing his hand on Cal's arm.

Cal pulled away, causing a stab of pain to shoot through his shoulder.

"I can't stay," he said and got into his plane. When he called 'Clear,' Tate stepped away. Cal taxied the plane to the runway and lifted off.

Once he was airborne, he turned his plane toward Big Canyon Rim, the range where his father had been shot. Moments with his dad flooded Cal's mind as he cruised overhead, remembering his parents arguing before John Jamison had ridden out to mend some fences – it was the last day he saw his dad alive…

"Someday, I'll find that son-of-a-bitch," Cal promised and banked the plane toward Tumalo.

CHAPTER 7

CAL TOOK A DEEP breath and sighed when he landed the Cessna on the Double J airstrip. This place felt more like home whenever he returned.

He grabbed his belongings and walked toward the house. Alfred, Winnie's tuxedo cat, followed him. The animal, with the distinctive markings, was always waiting when Cal landed his plane.

As he passed the stables, Cal heard a horse whinny. He walked in and set his stuff near a bale of hay. Alfred now sat in front of the gate of one stall and cleaned his black and white face with a front paw.

Bravo's head came out over a gate - a gray dun Kiger stallion Cal had adopted in 2007 while on leave from Iraq. It was another time in Cal's life he'd rather forget, but then, Glenn had insisted he needed a distraction.

"Hey, boy," Cal said in a soothing voice to the horse. "Are you missing me?"

He went inside and ran his hand down the black dorsal stripe along the horse's back, which was striking against his coat. These horses have deep chests and short backs, and were known to be sure-footed and intelligent.

Glenn had begun adopting Kiger horses since 2000. A few years later, he'd decided to start his own herd to breed and sell these magnificent animals. Now, Cal and Micco would be helping with Glenn's herd.

Cal scratched the horse's long neck. Bravo was fifteen hands high, strong muscled, with a mark of a white pyramid on his forehead. He'd been a handful at first, but with Micco's help, they tamed him for saddle riding.

Looking at his watch, Cal decided he'd better get going. "We'll go for a ride later," he said and left the stable.

AS HE ENTERED THE house, Cal was thankful for the smell of fresh coffee.

"I'm home," he called out as he kicked the door shut with his foot. He set his box and guitar down next to the rifle rack, then removed his boots.

"We're in the kitchen," Winnie said.

It did Cal's heart good when he saw both his grandparents in their usual seats at the old rustic pine table that had been in their family for years. He'd been told the story of how it had come on a ship in 1871 from New Orleans to Astoria, which carried his early ancestor, Helen Ahem. She met Callum Jamison there. They were married and came to the homestead near Crooked River. The table came with her. It's wood was cut against the grain and had a dark wax tobacco stain.

"Get yerself a cup of coffee and come sit a spell," Glenn said in his gruff voice.

Cal poured the dark liquid into a mug with a coyote logo and sat in the high-backed chair of the same wood next to his grandfather. His grandmother had given him that mug when he was young, saying that the coyote was his animal spirit.

"How's the homestead?" Glenn asked with a wistful look in his eyes.

"Pretty much the same as the last time I was there. Mom and Jack were gone, so I got my stuff and left before they got back. Micco's on his way now." He took a sip and then added, "Wes asked after you."

Glenn nodded and smiled. "He's a good man."

"I told Tate you were home, so he might come by sometime. I hope that's okay."

Glenn smiled. "That young man reminds me so much of your dad."

"We thought Micco might like the large room above the garage," Winnie said smiling. "I cleaned it up a bit and took some clean linens." She smiled and added, "I put some beers in the refrigerator."

Cal laughed. "Thanks. He's going to feel like royalty up there – never had a place of his own before."

"I gotta go check my chickens," Winnie said and left the room.

Glenn said, "I appreciate him coming here to help me with the Kigers."

"Micco said he could help you set up a website to sell those horses. You can reach a larger buyer's market that way."

"I know nothin' about computers and that stuff, so more power to him." Glenn took a sip of his coffee, then added, "I'll need you two to also watch my small head of Belted Galloway cattle until I'm back on my feet. They're in the back pasture now. I didn't want any Black Angus here on my ranch – not like at the old homestead."

Cal knew why his grandfather had chosen that breed when he began his herd at Double J. He'd bought a bull and two cows that were for sale over in Burns. The cattle were mostly black, with a wide band of white hair around their bellies. The breed originated in the Galloway Region of northern Scotland – the country where their ancestors came from.

"More coffee, son?" Glenn asked.

Cal could see his grandfather was getting tired. "No, thanks anyway," he said and took his empty cup to the sink. Through the kitchen window he saw his friend's truck pull in.

"Micco's here. I'm going to help him unpack."

THE ROOM ABOVE THE three-car garage was one large area with a small kitchenette and bathroom. An island with two stools separated the kitchen from the rest of the room. To the back, on one side, was a bed and night stand. The opposite wall had a desk and a couple of bookcases. In the middle was a couch and coffee table.

After the two men had carried up all of Micco's things, Cal watched as his friend set up his desk first. He was connecting his computer and printer as Cal got two of their favorite beers out of the fridge – Black Butte Porter from the local Deschutes Brewery.

Looking around the room, Cal said, "It's rustic, but—"

"Rustic?" Micco held his arms out wide. "Hell, this is more space than the entire old bunkhouse. I'm going to like living here."

"Remember the barracks we had at boot camp?" Cal said laughing. "It was about this size."

"San Diego was the first time I'd ever been to California – or seen the Pacific."

"Me, too."

A beep was heard as Micco booted up the computer.

"I'm definitely going to need a faster Wi-Fi here—" He stopped when he saw the look on Cal's face. "You okay?"

Cal sat on the couch and said, "I've been thinking…Forces Recon is what I know – it's what I was trained for and what I do best."

Micco took his beer and sat next to his friend. "And you're damned good at your job. What's brought this up?"

"I've been thinking about Glenn…"

"Ah," Micco said and leaned back. "Well, being a Marine is a good thing, but you do know how to run a ranch, too."

"At least it'll give me something to do now," Cal said, relaxing a bit. "I can't stand being idle."

CHAPTER 8

IT WAS PAST MIDNIGHT. The campfire was starting to burn down. Located deep in the forest, Luther was talking to his horse, Champ, before retiring for the night. This was a ritual he always did when he hunted alone with his horse.

"I saw the tracks of a large herd of elk this morning," he said as he checked the animal's tie. He'd used some hay string on the rope's end as an emergency breakaway attached to the picket line. That way, if Champ needed to pull away, he wouldn't hurt himself.

He stroked the Cob's neck, then scratched him under the flat red halter. "We'll see if I can fill our tag tomorrow."

Luther walked back to the campfire. He sat down on a stump nearby and poured another shot of Jack Daniels into his favorite blue-speckled enamel mug he'd had for years. Sadly, he noticed the bottle was almost empty.

"They were over by that range I walked along two days ago," he said out loud. He took a sip and added, "There was an enormous five-point buck, but he was too far away to get in a shot."

Coyotes started howling in the far distance. Luther took another sip, then continued, "I wish old Duke was here, but when hunting elk in Oregon, it's not allowed." The dog was a Bluetick Coonhound Luther rescued, which he usually took hunting for bobcat and cougars. He shook his head realizing that if anyone saw him, they'd think he was nuts, talking to himself.

Luther thought of his last mission in the Army – the one that gave him nightmares. His team had surveyed the compound they thought only contained a terrorist cell, but later learned there had been a few civilian casualties. He never forgave himself for that mistake and it was the last mission he'd led before retiring.

He looked over and saw Champ was paying no attention. "Yep, I think I'm going crazy – talking to a damned horse." He laughed, took the last sip of the golden liquid, then added, "But, you're a good listener, old boy."

The full moon rose overhead as Luther made sure the fire was extinguished, then he got up and stretched. After riding all day, his back was sore. He went into his tent, turned on the LED lantern and sat down on the cot. Ever since he was injured in that fire a year ago, his back couldn't handle sleeping on the ground.

Visions of the Sisters Rodeo last June popped into his head. He looked down at his belt buckle, which he always wore now to prove he was the Bull-Riding Champion. He loved the sport, but knew it would be his last. His body just couldn't take the beating anymore.

Pulling his pack out, he started looking through the investigator's file again. Photos of the charred building filled him with panic and he found it hard to breathe as he relived the incident in his mind.

Champ was snorting, which Luther ignored. Quickly jotting some notes on a blank sheet of paper, he wrote down each step he remembered as he entered that burning warehouse - before he'd been knocked out. After he noted taking off his mask to help Jeremy, he now recalled the smell of burning plastic. It was like another smell he knew from his military days – the odor of C-4 explosives.

Ever since the previous Fourth of July, something had started bothering him. It was the smell from the kids' firecrackers that triggered his brain. Riley, his son, had put a string into a plastic bucket and lit it. Those short blasts and heated polyethylene odor seemed to cause some of Luther's memory to return. The flashes were coming now like a camera shutter clicking in his mind. But he still hadn't been able to grasp the meaning of it – until now.

Suddenly, he remembered that he'd seen some sort of device on the forklift's propane tank. That's what had been missing in his report. He noted these recollections, convinced now that the fire was caused by arson.

Luther heard Champ squeal. Then, a noise came just outside of his tent. He quickly shoved the papers back into his backpack and stowed it under his cot. Then, he grabbed his rifle and unzipped the tent flap half way. Looking out into the darkness, the moon cast the only light.

"Who's there?" he called and totally unzipped the opening. As he stepped out, a shot rang out.

Luther brought his rifle up to his hip, but it was too late. A full-sized cougar fell at his feet. Champ broke his tie and ran away. Luther was about to chase after his horse, but a twig snapped behind him.

"What the—" he said as he turned, but stopped and lowered his rifle as a man wearing camo gear and carrying a sniper rifle came out of some bushes into the dim light.

"Luther," the man said, smiling. "You're going to wish that big cat got to you first..."

CHAPTER 9

THE NEXT MORNING, JAMIE and Mary were in the kitchen at the Greeves' small family ranch, making sandwiches for Jamie's kids' lunches.

"I'm glad I took time off work while you're here," Jamie said to her sister.

"I know how much you love your job."

"Yes, working for the Trial Court Administrator has its perks and I've learned so much. Also, it keeps me busy while the kids are in school."

Looking out the window at the old barn with the faded red paint, Mary said, "Dad always loved this place." She laughed and added, "He called it the Creswell Ranch, even though it only consisted of five acres. I'm glad you kept the name all these years."

"Luther didn't want to change it. Dad always thought of himself as a cowboy, even though he was an Architectural Historian. Mom loved it here, too." She placed the sandwiches into the bags. "Remember how Dad wore chaps when he rode old Buck?"

"That was your favorite buckskin horse. I learned to ride on him, too, but I refused to wear chaps!"

The women looked at each other and laughed with tears running down their faces as they shared remembrances of their childhood that never really faded.

After a few moments, Mary wiped her eyes and said, "If we'd known you were pregnant your senior year, we never would have gone to New York." She had been only fourteen when her parents took her away from her sister because of a job her father took on the east coast.

"I know," Jamie said smiling, "but I didn't even know it then." She put an apple into each kid's bag. Then, she stopped and said, "I miss Mom and Dad."

The women silently shared the memory of losing their parents in a car accident back in 2008, but didn't say any more about it.

"Does Luther often go hunting alone?" Mary asked as she put a juice box into Josie's small insulated lunch bag.

Jamie looked sadly at her sister. "He's been moody lately. I know that fire last year did something to him – more than just his memory. I think he uses hunting to try to forget…"

"You never said why he joined the Army after Riley was born."

Jamie sighed. She'd kept this secret long enough. "It was because I had two miscarriages…and we needed the money."

Mary hugged her sister. "I'm so sorry. I didn't know." After a moment, she added, "But, now you have Josie."

"I DON'T WANT YOU in my room," the young boy said to his little sister as he came into the kitchen. "Mom, Josie won't leave me alone."

Jamie ruffled her son's hair, who was now, at age sixteen, as tall as she was. "She just wants to be with you, Riley."

"But, does she have to be there ALL the time?"

A smaller replica of Jamie stumbled into the room carrying a pink backpack. Josie was the spitting image of her mother, blonde and petite. She wore a plaid skirt and white T-shirt with heart appliqués, and her hair was pulled back into a ponytail.

"I think his room stinks," the little ten-year old said as she wrinkled her nose.

"Then, why do you bother coming in?" Riley whined as he sat on the floor and pulled on his cowboy boots. Like his dad, Riley dressed in Western wear most of the time.

"Because it bugs you," Josie said, smiling sweetly.

Jamie heard a vehicle coming up the main road.

"Here comes the school bus. You'd better get going." She gave each of the kids their lunch bags and hugged them. Josie ran out the door, but Riley sauntered up the lane. Duke, the old hound dog, chased after the kids as Jamie and Mary watched from the porch.

"Typical teenager, that boy," Jamie said, crossing her arms. "He hates school right now."

Mary stood by her sister. "That was us a long time ago," she said nostalgically as the bus pulled away and the big dog returned to the house.

Jamie put her arm around Mary's waist and hugged. "Yes, brings back more memories, huh?"

"Yep."

The two women walked back into the house.

Just then, they heard a horse whinny outside.

"That sounds like Champ," Jamie said excitedly. "Luther must be home."

She ran out of the house with Mary following.

Mary ran up to the horse and caught his lead rope. He was sweaty and struggled to breathe, so she led him to a water trough.

"Where's the truck and trailer?" Jamie asked, looking up the lane. "Where's Luther?"

She pulled out her cell phone from her back pocket and dialed Luther's number. "Voicemail," she said. "I'm calling Cal."

CHAPTER 10

CAL WAS IN THE Fly Fisher's Place in Sisters.

"You're going to like that Sage One fly rod," Kevin Fisk, the owner, said. He then pulled out a reel from a case near the register. "And, I think you should also get this Galvan T6 reel for it."

"I appreciate your help, Kevin. I've been using Dad's equipment for years, but thought maybe it was time to try something new."

"His Scott G Series fly rod is still one of the best. I remember when John bought it and the Hardy reel. He and I went to the Middle Deschutes for a test run."

"You fished with Dad?"

"Absolutely. I've had this store since 1990."

Cal smiled. "He and I fished for big Brown trout - he liked Paulina Lake best. Those fish are fighters."

"Especially when you catch a twenty-pound monster fish with a fly rod."

AFTER ADDING A COLLECTION of new flies to his purchase, Cal walked out of the shop.

He was excited about going to Sparks Lake later to do some fishing for cutthroat trout. It was a lake that only allowed fly fishing and some Midges were hatching. His trip to Paulina Lake the day before had resulted in a few lowly Kokanee salmon, little red fish that are a form of Sockeye salmon, but live entirely in freshwater. When he'd switched to a Beetle fly on the top, he caught some nice rainbow trout.

Cal's right shoulder pulled again when he laid the pole onto the back seat of his Jeep. When he began his therapy after returning home, he'd used fly casting in an attempt to restore the full motion of his arm and shoulder. Even though it still hurt at times, it was more of an annoying reminder now.

He sat for a moment and thought about how his relationship with his dad had been different from his brothers. John Jamison had always wanted Cal to take over the Jamison Ranch, but Cal's absence in the military put his brother, Jack, in that role.

Annoyingly, his cell phone rang. When he saw it was Jamie's number, he answered it.

"Cal, I need you to come to our ranch," Jamie's voice said anxiously. "Champ just came home…without Luther."

"Put him in his stall, but don't touch him, I'm on my way." Cal hung up, put his phone in his shirt pocket and started his Jeep.

CHAPTER 11

CAL HEADED TOWARDS JAMIE'S on Alfalfa Market Road, east of Pilot Butte. The butte was a volcanic lava dome that stood within Bend's city limits.

As he drove past Big Sky Park, a bank of dark clouds started to form to the north. The landscape opened up as he passed the farm where Glenn had purchased Odie, his Australian Shepherd.

Cal drove through the opened gate of the old Cresswell family ranch. Five Black Angus grazed in a small pasture and three horses stood in a field to the left. Passing the familiar white fence he'd helped Luther put up along the gravel driveway reminded him why he was there.

He parked his Jeep near the barn and walked in. Duke bayed and ran to him. Cal reached down and scratched the dog's long ears. When he saw Mary and Jamie, he realized he knew very little about Jamie's family.

"Thanks for coming," Jamie said as she ran up to him. "Luther's phone just goes to voicemail. I'm really worried – this isn't like him."

They walked over to where Mary stood. The dog sat down near Champ's stall door, as if protecting him.

"Where're the kids?" he asked.

"They just left for school," Mary said.

Cal looked at the frightened horse standing at the back of the stall. The piebald Cob was pawing the ground and his flanks were quivering. He wore only his halter with a lead line dangling from it.

Jamie's cell phone rang and she went outside to answer it.

"Mary," Cal said, "did you remove his saddle?"

"No, this is exactly as he was when he rode in. We called the vet."

He opened the gate and asked, "Would you mind holding his halter for me?"

"Sure," she said and slowly followed Cal into the stall.

He unhooked the lead rope, noticing the torn piece of baling twine on the end. As he walked around to the horse's left side, he gently laid his hands on Champ's neck. Then, he saw the blood-matted mane. Lifting the hair, he wasn't surprised to see puncture wounds.

"Easy boy," he said as he ran his hands over the horse's flank. He noticed some brambles tangled in the thick tail, but didn't touch them. Cal took one hand down Champ's left foreleg, but stopped just before the feathering around the hoof. Knowing what the maroon-colored flowers were, he took out his hanky and pulled a few from the hair.

"What is that?" Mary asked.

"Russian Knapweed – it can burn human skin. So, we'll need to use gloves to remove the rest." He carefully wrapped them and put the hanky into his jacket pocket.

Mary asked, "How long have you known Luther?"

"We met five years ago at the rodeo in Sisters. I learned that he liked to go fly fishing, which is my favorite sport."

He looked again at the horse and didn't like what he saw. "I wonder what made him leave Luther's camp," he said, dreading the images in his mind. Like Luther, he was also a hunter, so he knew that a horse wouldn't leave a campsite alone unless something drastic happened.

THE VET'S VAN, WITH a logo of a running horse on the side, pulled into the lane and parked near the barn. Doc Thompson, a tall, silver-haired man with wire-rimmed glasses, stepped out. He pulled his black bag from the back seat as Jamie came out of the house.

"Thank you for getting here so quickly," Jamie said. They entered the barn together and she introduced her sister.

Doc Thompson said, "I haven't seen you since you were a young teenager, before you left for New York."

"Yes," Mary said, smiling at the older man. "I'm just here visiting from Seattle."

Champ snorted, which caught the older man's attention.

"Hey, Cal. Good to see you again," the vet said as he walked into the stall. In a singsong voice, he began, "So, what has this sweet-tempered animal been up to—" Suddenly he stopped and quickly looked at Cal.

Cal nodded and was glad he heard a phone ringing in the house.

"Jamie, you'd better get that – it could be Luther." He nodded to Mary and she understood.

"I'll come with you," the younger sister said.

After the women left, Doc said, "What the hell happened here? And, where is Luther?"

"Luther's out hunting...Champ returned without his master." He paused for a second and added, "You saw them, too."

The vet nodded as he walked to the horse's left shoulder. "Yes, I didn't want to say anything in front of the women, but those wounds look like he was attacked by a large animal."

"Possibly a cougar?" Cal asked.

"Maybe." Looking more closely, he said, "These are claw and teeth marks, which penetrated the skin and muscle. I'll need to flush out the wounds to avoid scabs from forming or they can cause anaerobic bacteria to grow and cause infection." Doc Thompson opened his bag and went to work to clean the gashes.

CAL WENT TO THE house. When he looked at Jamie, he saw that her face wrought with fear. "Was that Luther on the phone?" he asked.

Jamie shook her head. "It was a co-worker at my office. She couldn't find a file on a case that is going to trial later this week."

"Do you know where Luther was going?" he asked.

She shook her head. "He never talks much about it."

Cal put his hand in his pocket and thought for a moment, then said, "I think I know where he might be."

"Can I come too?" Mary asked.

"You'd better stay here with Jamie."

When he saw Jamie's face, he smiled and added, "I'm sure he's okay. Something probably spooked Champ. I'll call you as soon as I find him."

On the way to his Jeep, once he was out of earshot, Cal called Micco.

"Get our horses loaded and make it fast. I'll meet you at the Alfalfa Store by the Feedin' Trough."

"What's up?" his friend asked.

"Luther may be in trouble."

CHAPTER 12

CAL POURED OVER A map as Micco drove his truck onto Route 20 heading east. The horse trailer trailed after them.

"You know we have GPS now…on our cell phones even," Micco said laughing.

"Yeah, but I still prefer a printed map."

Cal saw the landmark for the oldest Juniper tree dated back 1600 years on Horse Ridge. Then, when they passed a brown sign that said, 'Oregon Badlands,' he put the map away.

There were various dirt roads leading from the highway for 'Off Highway Vehicle' access used by many hunters. The old sign for the Millican Store with gas prices was still standing at elevation four thousand feet. The terrain surrounding it was dotted with big sagebrush and Juniper trees, as well as a few pine evergreens.

"Stop at Brothers," Cal said. "That's where Luther always went for breakfast before finding a campsite."

"How do you know that?" Micco asked.

"Luther is a creature of habit. After that, he probably went to the same area he talked about a few times."

Cal pulled out the handkerchief containing the petals he'd found on Luther's horse. "These are from Russian Knapweed. They were in Champ's hair."

"Hope that horse didn't eat any of those," Micco said. "They're toxic to horses. They can get what's called 'chewing disease,' which can cause death."

When they pulled up to the old 1912 Stage Stop, Cal was pleased when he saw that the post office and café were both open. "I'll go in and see if anyone saw Luther," he said.

As Cal got out, Micco went back to check the horses in the trailer. In the distance, the Pine Mountain range stood, with the Observatory on the peak.

CAL WALKED PASSED THE small post office on the left and into the empty store and restaurant. Round black stools sat before a wood slab counter and a big American flag was proudly displayed in front of a billboard with notices tacked up. A model rocket hung over a couple abandoned tables with dirty dishes - signs of possible hunters after breakfast. Noises from the kitchen came from the back.

He approached the cook, who was pulling a tray of chocolate chip cookies from the oven. "Hey, Grumpy, how've you been?"

"Callum Jamison, as I live and breathe!" the large man yelled in a Scottish accent. He had a few days' growth on his face and wore a soiled apron "How's Glenn doin' these days? I heard about him…"

"News travels fast. He's home again, mean as ever."

The cook laughed. "Not much gets that man down."

He pulled more cookie dough from a tall fridge. "What brings you this way? Hunting?"

"No," Cal said. "But, I'm looking for a friend who is – have you seen Luther Greeves?" He didn't want to alarm the man about Luther's possible disappearance.

Grumpy scratched his stubbly chin. "He came through five days ago. Haven't seen him since. Why're you looking for him?"

"His wife tried to call, but couldn't reach him, so I'm just checking in."

"Said he was going somewhere south of here."

"That's what I figured, but wanted to check with you first. You always know what's going on in these parts."

When Grumpy saw Cal eyeing the tray, he said, "Help yerself."

Cal grabbed two cookies from a tray and said, "Micco's with me. Thanks for your help."

"Any time. Tell that old geezer 'Hey' for me."

"Will do."

CHAPTER 13

AS CAL GOT IN beside Micco, he handed his friend a cookie.

"Gotta love Grumpy!" Micco said. "What'd he say?"

"Head back west on Route 20, then turn south on Fort Rock Road. We're going towards China Hat."

The cone-shaped formation had gotten its name because of its configuration. It was a volcanic butte in the Paulina Unit of the Deschutes National Forest, near the Newberry Volcano. It sat over sixty-five-hundred feet above the Ponderosa and Lodgepole Pine trees that provided cover for herds of Rocky Mountain elk.

They drove on the paved road, crossed a cattle guard and then the road turned into sand and gravel. Pine Mountain was to their left. The trees grew denser and the sunlight became dim in the green canopy overhead.

After a few miles, Cal pointed to a rustic pullout at the side of the road and said, "There's Luther's truck."

They stopped and got out. Looking inside, Cal could

see the coffee cups and food wrappers still on the passenger's seat and floor. Luther was never one to keep his rig clean. The gun rack and horse trailer were both empty.

Cal said, "Let's get our horses ready."

Bravo backed out of their trailer easily and Cal began saddling him. But, Micco's horse still didn't like trailers. The horse kicked the sidewalls and raised his head in protest.

"Easy, Isha," Micco cooed to his brown and white Paint. His mother had chosen that name when he was given the colt years ago – it meant 'trustworthy steed' in Northern Paiute.

They locked up their truck and headed west on horseback.

CHAPTER 14

AS THEY RODE, CAL checked the sandy soil for shod horse tracks. He saw some scat and cougar prints. After about three miles, he noticed the forest was getting thicker, with more underbrush, but he could see a ridge to the west.

When they came to a clearing, Micco pointed to a narrow column of smoke rising in the distance. "Over there," he said and they both kicked their horses into a gallop.

They came upon a small campsite and quickly dismounted.

"Luther," Cal called out, but there was no answer.

Micco found the area where Champ had been tethered. He noticed some bailing twine still tied to the picket line and there was dried blood on the ground. Cal joined him.

"That horse must've run over thirty miles from here to the ranch," Cal said.

As they walked toward the tent, they were surprised to see a dead cougar lying near the cold fire pit.

"Where's that smoke coming from that we saw earlier?" Micco asked.

"I don't know." Cal looked inside the tent while Micco checked the animal.

"This cat's been shot," Micco said.

When Cal came out of the tent, he saw signs of a struggle. "There's a lot of blood over here." He knelt down. "I don't think this is from the animal."

A gust of wind blew through the campsite. Cal's head came up sharply. "Smell that? Burning Juniper."

The two men ran toward a ridge nearby and saw the source of the smoke.

"Come on," Cal yelled.

WHEN CAL REACHED THE cause of the smoke, he stopped. A charred and lifeless body lay on top of the burning pyre of Juniper and Big Sagebrush, the diminishing flames pulsating around the burnt flesh. On the outer rim was some cheatgrass that hadn't burned yet, which was a major fire hazard in Oregon.

"Good God," Micco said as he joined Cal. Looking around, he added, "I hope this isn't Luther." He was about to reach toward the body, but Cal stopped him.

"I've seen enough bombings in the Middle East to know you don't touch burned bodies. We need to try to put out this fire as much as we can."

They hurriedly found large sticks nearby to push some of the burning branches away from the body, being careful to avoid the underbrush nearby.

"Call 911," Cal said to his friend.

Micco pulled out his cell phone and walked a short distance away, searching for a signal. "I'm going to have to go to that ridge we passed to get service."

"Wait for the authorities and lead them here."

Alone, Cal looked down at the blackened flesh and saw how the muscles had pulled the body into a fetal position. In spite of this, he caught sight of a large silver object – a belt buckle. He put a handkerchief over his mouth and nose to get a closer look. Then, he quickly pulled back. He'd been able to read enough of the engraving to know that this was Luther. Cal was with him at the last Sisters Rodeo when Luther won first place in the Bull Riding event.

Cal stood and looked around. He had a sense that he was being watched, an itchy feeling he would sometimes get when on a mission. The last time he had that feeling was in Afghanistan.

CHAPTER 15

IT WAS SOME TIME before CAL heard sirens in the far distance. He was in Luther's tent, looking for anything that could help him understand why this had happened. He'd found Luther's rifle lying just outside of the tent, but he didn't touch it.

Quickly, he went through Luther's jacket. He was surprised Luther hadn't been wearing it, considering the lower temps in this area at night. That told him that somehow his friend had been surprised. The only thing he found in one pocket was a receipt for a bottle of Jack Daniels and a can of Grizzly chew that was purchased at a liquor store before leaving Bend. Cal noted the address of the store and put it back in the pocket.

The rest of the tent contents were disheveled, but didn't look as if anyone had searched through Luther's belongings. Before handling any more evidence, Cal remembered the gloves he always carried in his coat pocket and put them on. When he picked up the sleeping bag hanging near the tent's floor, he spotted the blue backpack under the cot and pulled it out. Inside were papers and Luther's notes regarding the fire that he'd been injured in the prior year. Cal could hear voices now, so he quickly spread a few pages out on the cot and took a couple snapshots with his phone. He knew he was tampering with evidence, since this probably was a murder, but Luther was his friend. He placed the papers back into the bag and returned it where he'd found it.

JUST AS CAL STEPPED out of the tent, he heard Micco say, "Luther's camp is just over here…"

"Were you hunting with him?" a familiar voice with a bit of southern accent asked. Sheriff Scott Morrow, a tall, lanky man with salt and pepper hair, came around a large pine into the clearing. He stopped when he saw Cal standing near the dead cougar's body.

"Well, there's a sight you don't see every day," Morrow said.

Andy Shaw, a detective at the local sheriff's office and a friend of Cal's, joined them. He set his camera bag down and asked, "What the hell happened here?"

"The cat has a bullet in it," Micco said.

"Andy, we'll need to call the State Police to come process this animal," the sheriff said.

"I'll get Bateman on it." Andy pulled out his DSLR camera. "The fire truck's on its way," he told Cal, then started taking photos of the cougar's body and the campsite. Micco took him to where Champ had been tethered.

Deputy Rupert Bateman, a big guy with sandy hair, entered the campsite. He was carrying silver cases. The deputy stopped when he saw Cal. "Why're you here?" he asked gruffly.

Cal knew Bateman hated him, but never really knew why. He just figured the man was angry more at his parents for giving him that name and took it out on everyone else. The sheriff was the only one he allowed to call him by his given name.

"This isn't the worst of it," Cal said. "You're going to need the Medical Examiner."

"Right behind us," Morrow said, standing with his hands on his hips. "As Rupert asked, why are you here, Jamison?"

"I got a call from Jamie, Luther's wife," Cal told the sheriff. "His horse came home alone this morning. I knew Luther was hunting somewhere around here, so I offered to come look for him."

"Why didn't she call our office?" Morrow asked.

"It wasn't a murder then, just a missing friend," Cal said and turned to lead the way to Luther's body.

CHAPTER 16

THEY WALKED THROUGH THE brush, kicking up dust from the sandy soil as if they were walking on the moon. A lizard scurried across the path in front of them and the screech of a golden eagle flying overhead broke the silence.

"Prepare yourselves," Cal warned.

"When did you get here?" Andy asked him.

"Micco and I arrived a little less than an hour ago and tried to put the fire out."

When the men came up to the now smoldering bonfire, they stopped in their tracks. The smoke drifted eastward.

"My God," Andy said, covering his mouth and nose with his handkerchief from the stench of the charred body. "Who the hell is that?"

Cal said nothing.

Trying to ignore the nauseating smell, Morrow said, "Andy, take photos before any more evidence is contaminated."

As Andy captured the crime scene, a four-wheel-drive fire engine came up a nearby fire lane. Two men in full gear got out at the crime scene to determine what equipment they would need.

Captain Clark Dixon nodded to the sheriff, then said to the other firefighter, "Get your backpack pump and contain this before it spreads into the underbrush."

"On it, sir," the younger fireman replied.

As the two men worked, Dixon said, "This cheatgrass is so combustible around here and the Western juniper contains a highly flammable volatile oil. Whoever set up this pyre knew what they were doing."

The others stood back while the firefighters worked quickly to suppress what flames were left and prevent a wildfire, which was prevalent in those woodlands of Oregon.

When Dixon declared the area was contained and the smoke was clearing, Sheriff Morrow said to his deputy, "Rupert, better call the Slumber Mortuary."

"Why a funeral home?" the older deputy asked.

"The Deschutes County Medical Examiner always prefers using a mortuary vehicle to keep ambulances free for the living."

JUST THEN, THEY ALL turned as a black Harley Davidson motorcycle came up the fire lane with a sidecar containing a fawn-colored Shepherd dog, wearing doggles and a skull and cross-bone bandana.

Andy leaned over and said to Cal, "That's Dr. Jordan Hansen, our medical examiner. She's new – only been here six months."

Bateman snickered and said, "Her dog's riding shotgun."

"Get your hands off my body!" the woman called out as she got off the bike.

She was slender, with curves in all the right places in her dark blue jumpsuit. As she removed her helmet, her long ginger-colored hair fell loosely over her shoulders. She possessed an air of confidence that suggested she could take control of any situation her profession might bring her way.

The men were stunned.

The dog jumped out of the sidecar.

Sheriff Morrow finally broke the silence. "I see you brought your dog, Dr. Hansen."

"Yes, Tut is a well-trained cadaver dog." She removed the animal's doggles and looked at her watch. Then, she added, "And, as you know, Sheriff, he's been very helpful to your office on many crime scenes."

"Why's he called Tut?" Bateman asked. "He's not a mummy."

The woman smiled and said, "I named him King Tut after President Hoover's Belgian Malinois."

"Rupert," Morrow said to his deputy, "I told you to go call the mortuary. And, tell the State Police about that cat."

The big man grumbled as he lumbered off back toward the squad car.

The other men turned and watched as the woman tied her hair back before she took a black bag out of the vintage bike's saddlebag.

Then, Dr. Hansen walked over and knelt down near the charred body. She took her time visually examining the victim's posture, leaning in closer as she noted some abnormal markings on the extremities.

After a bit, she stood and looked at the surrounding area for clues to help her analyze this victim's death.

"This is my first burning bush case…," she said as she

glanced at the men standing around her. "I've heard stories about how a body could disappear out here like this and never be found."

The dog came over and stood near her.

"Tut, seek," she said as she put on a pair of Latex gloves and went back to examining the body.

The dog sniffed around a bit, then went off toward the road near where the fire engine was parked.

Andy followed the dog.

"Can we get an estimated time of death?" Morrow asked.

"I can't even venture a guess about that now," the ME said. "I'll know more after the autopsy."

Bateman returned, but immediately ran to a nearby tree and vomited.

"He's contaminating my crime scene!" Dr. Hansen shouted.

The sheriff went over to check on his deputy.

Cal watched as the doctor took a pair of tweezers from her bag, picked up a fragment of burned cloth that lay on the edge of the firepit and placed it in an evidence bag.

He didn't say anything but he'd been with his friend when he bought that red-plaid flannel shirt at one of the sporting goods stores in Bend. Luther always said he liked to wear red when hunting so he wouldn't be mistaken for a deer in the woods.

He looked away and took a deep breath. Then, Cal turned and asked, "Is there any way to tell if he suffered?"

Dr. Hansen stood. "I'm afraid I cannot say just yet." Then, she placed her hand on his arm and said, "If this was your friend, I'm sorry for your loss."

IT WAS SOME TIME before the mortuary van arrived on the same fire lane, a logo 'For the Rest of Your Life' was written under the funeral home name.

"The meat wagon's here," Bateman yelled.

The mortician was tall and thin, dressed all in black.

The deputy walked over to the lanky man and asked, "Why use 'Slumber' for your business name?" He chuckled and added, "That's kind of catchy in your line of work."

The mortician looked embarrassed and explained, "It's our family name." He then pulled out a stretcher from the van.

A young man got out of the van's passenger's seat, took a body bag from the back of the vehicle and joined the doctor.

"We got here as fast as we could," he said to the doctor, "but some cattle were stranded on one of the roads." Looking down at the pyre, he said, "Wow, we got ourselves a real barbecue here."

"Respect!" Cal said sharply.

Dr. Hansen could tell she'd have to handle this crime scene with kid gloves. She looked at her colleague, then stood and said, "The people in our profession use humor to maintain our perspective and sanity."

She introduced the striking blond man standing next to her. "Peter Edwards is my new assistant."

"Hi all," Peter said. He looked at Cal and added, "Sorry, sir." Then, he began taking photos of the crime scene.

Clearing her throat to get back to business, the doctor affirmed, "This is going to be difficult to ID, considering the condition of the body. But, I'd say we have a male - about mid-to-late thirties. I'll know more when I get him on the table."

She asked the men standing around her, "Who found

the body?"

"I did," Cal said. "I'm Cal Jamison." He pointed to the body and added, "This man is - was Luther Greeves."

"How the hell do you know that?" the sheriff asked.

"That's his rodeo belt buckle."

The doctor said, "Well, I'm going to make damned sure before we notify any next of kin."

Then, she nodded to the mortician and Peter.

The two men carefully lifted the charred body onto the opened bag laying on the stretcher and zipped it shut. They solemnly loaded everything onto the waiting van.

"Please take the body to the hospital morgue," the examiner said. "I'll do the autopsy there."

"You mean we get to do it this time?" Peter asked excitedly.

Morrow said, "Protocol is to send suspicious death cases to the State Lab in Clackamas."

Dr. Hansen explained. "Before I left, I heard that their autopsy room is locked down right now due to a mass fatality event in Portland."

They all watched in silence as the van drove away.

ANDY RETURNED, WITH TUT following him. "I found tire tracks back there," he said, pointing to a ridge in the distance. "I'll get a casting before we leave."

"Get some photos of the firepit," the sheriff told Andy, "now that the body is gone."

After Andy was finished, Dixon began going through the remnants of the firepit. Suddenly, the firefighter stood up and yelled, "Oh, hello!"

Morrow went over to him and asked, "What's up?"

"We have the point of ignition." Dixon knelt and pointed to a small distinct trail of ashes. Andy took more photos.

"This was started with a road flare," Dixon added.

"A lot of hunters use them to start campfires," Cal said.

ON A SMALL RISE, over a thousand yards to the east, the man was sprawled before a tripod, where his long-range rifle, commonly known as the Arctic Warfare Magnum, was mounted. He'd chosen this particular position with his back to the sun so that he could watch through his high-power scope.

Being careful so no light would catch on the scope's lens, he reveled in all the activity around the pyre he'd meticulously built to exact his revenge. He had hoped that Luther wasn't found so quickly, but he grew excited as the medical team extracted what remained of the man he'd hunted for years. It took him more time than he'd wanted and he felt the satisfaction of a mission accomplished – but he wasn't finished yet.

He smiled. Now he knew what all the other players looked like.

CHAPTER 17

DR. JORDAN HANSEN WALKED into the hospital morgue. The light was on and the room cold and sterile with the familiar strong chemical smell. Today, there was a pungent odor of charred flesh. Her assistant was there setting up the necessary tools for her autopsy of the body on the table.

"Hi, Peter," she said. "Thanks for getting our victim ready."

"I named him John Doe, since we don't have an ID yet," the young man said. "Is there a way to identify all the John and Jane Does we get in the morgue – like Doe1, Doe2?"

She laughed and said, "Hopefully, we're able to identify each body before the Does are released."

He watched as she walked to the desk and set her pack and helmet down next to the corpse's file. Then, as usual, she looked over her notes from the crime scene.

Peter chuckled as he finished laying out the instruments. "The smell in here reminds me of a hayride and wiener roast we had after homecoming in high school. I almost went to second base with Molly Walters on that ride."

"Those were fun times," she said remembering her own homecomings of past.

Jordan walked to the coat rack near the door. She hung up her leather jacket and put on the waiting lab coat.

"I am sorry for the reason we're doing this here, instead of the State Lab," she said. "I did all of my own autopsies back in San Diego. Since I came to Oregon, the laws have sometimes kept me from that part of my job that I love."

"You like doing these kinds of cases?" Peter asked.

She looked at the young man. Peter was a medical student there on a fellowship, but she was training him for a new program of medical death investigators she was developing.

"I love finding answers," she replied.

"Our crispy critter is ready and waiting," he said.

Jordan smiled as she pulled on some gloves and went to the stainless-steel table. "I see you've found your own way to cope. But we have to be careful not to be too callus when others are with us – they don't see our work the same way we do."

Looking down at the burn victim, Jordan took a moment before beginning her preliminary exam on the contorted body. This was something she'd done since her first autopsy out of respect for the dead.

"Why does he look like that, Dr. Hansen?" Peter asked. "This is my first major burn case."

"That position is what is usually described as a pugilistic posture. His arms and legs are in what looks like a fighter's stance, due to the pulling effect of the muscles and tendons shortening as a response to the cooking of the flesh."

"That's so weird, but fascinating."

As she visually scanned the body, she noticed something and pointed to the left arm of the body. "See this? Fractures of extremity bones – in this case, his radial and ulnar bones - were fractured due to this contortion, which is common in severe burn victims."

Jordan looked at her assistant and added, "This positioning develops in bodies regardless of whether they are alive or dead when exposed to a heat source."

"Oh, I hope this guy was dead."

"Me, too. Now, please take both anterior and posterior full-body digital X-rays, as well as lateral views."

"Roger that."

"And, call the hospital's Forensic Photographer to get images of his mouth."

"Alright! I like working with Aleshia."

Jordan laughed. "Yes, she is beautiful. We'll compare her digital files to this man's dental records I asked for."

"How did you know which dentist to call?"

"A man at the crime scene thought he knew the victim. It will save time in identifying our John Doe."

CHAPTER 18

AS MICCO AND CAL walked toward the sheriff's office in Bend, Cal said, "I just wish we had more to go on about Luther's death."

"You're still sure it was him?"

Cal nodded. "He never went anywhere without that buckle."

"After this, we've got to get back to the ranch. There's a load of hay arriving."

With his phone in his hand, Cal said, "I have a confession."

Micco stopped in the parking lot and looked at his friend.

"I handled Luther's jacket and took photos of some papers he had in his tent," Cal said softly.

"Well, I wouldn't mention that to the sheriff right now."

"I'm going to have to say something – my prints are going to be there."

As the two men went in, the familiar smell of burnt coffee was the first thing Cal noticed. He'd spent his high school summers there working as a volunteer.

Sheriff Morrow, Andy, and Rupert Bateman were looking over an evidence board. Images of Luther's charred body and the campsite were the principal focus.

"I can't imagine anyone wanting to harm Luther Greeves," Andy said. "He was such a nice guy."

"We still don't know if it was Luther," the sheriff said. "I'm waiting for the ME's call."

When Cal closed the door, Bateman yelled, "You two again?"

"I was in—" Cal started, but stopped when he saw Andy shake his head. "I just thought I could help…since I used to work here as a cadet."

"That was when you were a sniveling kid, still in high school," Morrow laughed, then a stern look came over face. "This is official business—"

Cal took out his handkerchief and opened it. "I found these on Luther's horse – after Champ ran back to the ranch." He handed the cloth to the sheriff. "This Knapweed is what helped me find Luther's camp. Champ also had claw marks on his body, which Doc Thompson can confirm."

He handed the evidence to Andy.

Bateman laughed. "These are just weeds – nothing to do with the case—"

"I know that Luther was looking into the plastics building fire last year," Cal cut in. "And it's a coincidence that he died in a fire."

"I don't believe in coincidences," Morrow said.

"Me neither," Cal agreed. "But, before you got to the campsite, I looked around his tent."

"You what?" Morrow yelled.

Seeing the fire investigator's report on the board, Cal quickly added, "Luther recently told me that he had started to regain a little of his memory. It started when his kids put some firecrackers into a bucket that had a little motor oil left inside. When the bucket started to burn, that smell triggered something he'd recognized from that fire."

Morrow and Andy looked at each other. "That's what his note said," the sheriff said.

"We found notes at the crime scene—" Andy started, then stopped when his boss glared at him.

Cal sighed. "There are so many arson cases that never get solved."

"Who said the Hawks Plastics fire was arson?" Bateman growled.

"Just a lucky guess," Cal said, smiling. "Speaking of fires, do you know yet what type of flare was used to start that pyre near China Hat?"

"Dixon said they're still looking into it," Morrow said, then he seemed angry with himself for divulging case information. "I forgot – you don't work here anymore."

Andy quickly added, "The State Police Game Warden called earlier and said the bullet recovered that killed the cougar was a .338 Lapua."

Cal shot a glance at Micco. "That's a sniper's bullet."

A phone rang on one of the desks and Bateman picked it up. He listened for a moment, then said, "Thanks for letting us know," and hung up. He looked at the men standing around him and grinned, "That was the hot ME. She wants us to come to the hospital morgue."

Morrow picked up his hat from his desk.

When Bateman began gathering his things, the sheriff said to his deputy, "Rupert, you stay here to man the office."

Cal looked at Micco and his friend nodded, aware that he'd be going alone to help with the hay delivery.

"Can I come along, Sheriff?" Cal asked hopefully. When he saw the disapproving look on Morrow's face, he added, "Luther was my friend."

CHAPTER 19

IN THE HOSPITAL MORGUE, Dr. Hansen was dictating into a headset when the men arrived. Her assistant, Peter, and a beautiful African-American woman stood off to one side. The woman had the body of a ballerina and was holding a large camera with a flash attachment.

"I have finished my preliminary examination," the medical examiner said, "and the dental records confirm that this is the body of Luther Greeves, age thirty-six. The final cause of death is yet to be determined…"

She looked up at the sheriff and Cal standing near the head of the examination table and turned off the microphone. "Thank you for coming, gentlemen."

Cal took in a deep breath trying to tamp down his anger when he saw Luther's charred body lying under the sheet on the steel table. X-ray films hung on the Illuminator box on the wall to the right. Then, his gaze landed on the belt buckle laying on a smaller table.

"You have some evidence?" Sheriff Morrow asked.

"Yes. Because of Mr. Jamison's presumptive identification, I took the liberty of locating Luther Greeves' dentist. The teeth on this body match the radiographs we received. All of the third molars had been removed, except tooth number seventeen, the lower left third molar. There is a bridge implant over the missing tooth number eighteen and the second molar. And, there's a missing number twenty-one, the first premolar, in that same area."

She pointed to her staff and said, "You know my assistant, Peter. And, this is Aleshia Granado, my Forensic Photographer."

Andy smiled when he noted Aleshia's Nikon D800 digital single-lens camera and went to stand near her.

"Do you have a time of death yet?" Morrow asked impatiently.

She shook her head and said, "That's hard to determine and you know I don't like to guess. We'll have to wait for my full autopsy."

Dr. Hansen lifted the sheet to reveal the torso.

"Good lord," Andy groaned. "Why didn't he try to roll off that fire?"

She looked toward Cal for a moment, then said, "He could have been dead before he was put there." She pointed to the upper arms and chest areas. "See these wounds?"

Cal stepped in closer, bent over the body, then looked up sharply at the ME. "Knife marks."

"Yes. I was surprised at first, too. There are several stab wounds."

"He was tortured?" Morrow asked the examiner.

"I don't know yet." Seeing Cal's reaction to this news, she covered the body again.

"We need to notify his family," Morrow said.

Andy nodded and said, "Luther's parents live in Klamath Falls. The sheriff there will inform them."

"Thank you, Dr. Hansen," Morrow said and he started to leave. He stopped and asked Cal, "Are you coming?"

"I need a moment."

"I'll stay with him, sir," Andy said. "I need to be here to witness the autopsy."

"I'll escort you out, Sheriff," Peter said, and the two men left.

As the door closed, Cal stood solemnly, unable to pull himself away. "Dr. Hansen—"

"Please, call me Jordan."

"Jordan, I've seen marks like this before," he began, "in the service." He didn't add that he'd used similar tactics himself on special missions. "Those points were strategically inflicted to cause the most blood loss." He paused, then added, "I agree, Luther was probably dead before he was burned."

She nodded and said, "I'll know more after further examination." Jordan donned a pair of gloves, removed the sheet and continued to look over the body.

"Aleshia, please take some close-ups of these marks," Jordan instructed as she measured the knife marks with a ruler. The camera's flash went off numerous times.

Andy said to the young photographer, "Hi, I'm Andy Shaw, Detective for the County Sheriff. I also take photos at our crime scenes, so I'll make sure you get copies of this case."

She smiled and asked, "What type of camera do you use?"

"A Canon 5D Mark III." Andy added, "Your camera has more megapixel sensors. I'm jealous."

Aleshia laughed and returned to snapping photographs.

There were numerous similar wounds all along the body's arms and legs.

After a while, Jordan said, "It looks like these cuts were made with a double-edged, non-serrated blade."

"Like a dagger?" Cal asked.

"Possibly."

Jordan came back to stand by his side and watched the young photographer work.

Aleshia asked the doctor to move the sheet a little more so she could take closeup photos of the torso.

"Why does Luther look so contorted?" Andy asked.

"A burning body is like a hot dog on a stick…" Aleshia began. "It contracts in the heat and the skin can burst open—" She stopped and looked at the two men. "Too much?"

Jordan said, "Sometimes we forget…a sense of humor helps us to cope with it all."

When the camera's flash went off again, something on the body caught Jordan's eye. "Wait a minute," she said and pulled a lighted magnifier over to get a closer look. Then, she took a pair of teethed forceps and pulled out a tiny piece of metal.

"Is that a knife tip?" Cal asked.

"Could be. It was in the victim's right rib cage." The item made a metallic pinging sound when she dropped it into a glass evidence jar.

"Could that mean the attacker was left-handed?" Cal asked, even though he guessed the answer.

"Possibly. Like I said, I'll have to wait for my full autopsy, which I will finish in a few moments…after you leave," she said to Cal.

Just then, Peter returned and Jordan asked him to take the sample to the hospital's lab. Andy and Aleshia stood at the back of the room, talking about photography.

Jordan took off her gloves and walked to the desk.

Cal followed her across the cold room. "Jordan," he said, "that's a Hebrew name."

She smiled and shook her head. "Dad really wanted a boy."

"What brought you here?" he asked.

As she sat down, she shrugged and said, "I guess I was looking for something different."

Cal filed this new information away in his mind, knowing she was holding something back about her personal life. But then, in his job he learned that everyone had secrets. He knew his. Now, he wondered what secret Luther might have had worth getting him tortured.

As he stood by her, he hoped that later he'd get a chance to see her report. When she opened the pack lying on the desk, a photo of her Belgian Shepherd fell to the floor. Cal picked it up and asked, "Where did you get your dog?"

She took the photo and smiled. "Tut was from a litter in San Diego, being trained for the Navy SEALs. But I got to him first." She looked up at Cal and asked, "What branch were you in?"

"Marines." He didn't go into detail of what his job was. But, since she'd brought it up, he added, "I started Basic Training in San Diego at the Recruit Depot by the airport. Then, I was sent to Camp Pendleton."

"I loved San Diego. My favorite lunch place was on Coronado Island at a little restaurant in the marina."

Cal laughed and said, "One time, when I was off duty there, I visited the old 1888 hotel. In the gift shop, I bought a sweet flask like Hemingway used." He looked at the redhead and asked, "Were you from California originally?"

"No, Nebraska. I got my medical degree in Omaha." Jordan stopped and looked away. "After my residency, I went to Hawaii with some friends to celebrate. My parents died while I was gone." She turned back to Cal and added, "It was a home invasion - the case was never solved. That's when I went into Forensics. I vowed to do all I could for families who lose loved ones to get answers they need to find closure. After I became certified, I worked in various places...until San Diego."

Cal could tell there was something else there in her past she was evading, but he didn't press it. "I'm sorry to hear about your parents," he said.

Jordan put her hand on the picture frame and said, "Tut's the only family I have now."

"I lost my dad when I was fifteen." He didn't add that they both had unsolved cases in their pasts. "I still have a big family, but we don't see eye to eye on many things."

"At least you have a family."

Just then, Jordan's cellphone started ringing and buzzing simultaneously. She brushed her left breast with her arm and smiled.

Cal looked at her and asked, "You keep your phone in your bra?"

"Yes. It keeps my hands free when I'm working." Jordan ignored the call and continued smiling.

"Aren't you going to answer it?" he asked.

"No. I'll check it later...the vibration is more fun."

"Well, I'd best be going." 7Cal smiled and started for the door just as Peter returned.

CHAPTER 20

"WE BETTER GET STARTED," Dr. Hansen said as she returned to the autopsy table.

Andy stood to one side to observe.

"I'm sorry if this is difficult for you," Jordan said to the deputy, "especially if this was also your friend."

Andy shrugged. "He was more Cal's friend than mine."

The examiner adjusted the headset on her head again and turned on the microphone. Then, she donned a clean pair of gloves and a clear shield to protect her face.

Picking up a ruler from the instrument table, she dictated, "This is the full autopsy of Luther Greeves. A knife used on the body was approximately seven-eighths of an inch wide, possibly a type of dagger. And the wounds were inflicted to create venous bleeding – the main arteries appear to have been avoided to prevent too rapid blood loss."

As Jordan laid the ruler back onto the tray, she was reminded of Cal Jamison. She decided to find out more about the man when this was all over.

She then opened the body by making an upside-down Y incision over the sternum and onto the abdomen, just below the rib cage bilaterally.

Peter handed her a bone saw, which ran on compressed air.

Jordan examined the chest first and probed puncture wounds as they traversed into the body cavities, measuring and dictating at every step. Next, she explored the abdomen; each organ was removed, weighed and inspected for injury.

"I'll record any genetic or surgical abnormalities on my chart," Peter said. "Later I will probe the knife wounds on the extremities and make those notes, as well."

Jordan looked over at Andy and turned off her microphone. "It's okay of you feel sick – these exams aren't for the faint of heart."

"I'm good," Andy said. "This isn't my first autopsy."

She smiled, remembering she now lived in rodeo country. "Ah, I see you're gaining our sense of humor."

The examiner pointed towards the body and explained, "The last area to examine is the head and neck. The brain must be inspected for bleeding or trauma. If there are any wounds to the neck, I will open and explore with a midline incision. Understand?"

Andy took a deep breath and nodded.

Hours later, after the autopsy was completed, Andy asked, "Do you have cause of death?"

Jordan said, "I've taken blood samples from the liver and will have to wait for the CO test results. That will give me levels of carbon monoxide. I can usually talk the hospital's lab staff into getting them back in a day or so. All toxicology has to go to the State Medical Examiner's lab and can take months to get results."

"What about time of death?"

"The time of death is always the time at which the body was discovered. But, the actual time will likely be either before or after the body was placed on the pyre. That's as specific as I can be for now."

Aleshia had packed up her camera equipment and went up to Andy. "I'll walk you out, Mr. Shaw."

"Please, call me Andy."

The two left the room.

"I'll take the samples to the lab," Peter said to the doctor and followed the other two.

Alone, Jordan looked at the corpse's neck again. On a hunch, she put on some gloves and made a lengthwise incision with a scalpel and scissors. Quickly, she stepped back from the table.

"Good Lord."

CHAPTER 21

CAL AND SHERIFF MORROW were alone in the County Sheriff's Office – a rare opportunity. Morrow had just brought a couple cups of coffee to his desk.

"Where is everyone?" Cal asked as he sat in a chair next to the sheriff and laid his black baseball cap on the desk.

"Andy and Rupert went to the State Police office to do a comparison on that tire casting made at the crime scene."

"You know Rupert hates to be called by his first name."

"Yeah," the sheriff said with a crooked smile. "That's why I do it…to keep him humble."

"There's nothing humble about that man."

"I see you're wearing the cap you had in school."

Cal wiped some dust from the bill. "Yeah, I found it when I went back to the Jamison Ranch to get my stuff."

He looked at the older man's weathered face, his hair just brushed the collar of his tan uniform shirt. They'd known each other for years. Cal knew Scott Morrow was born in Arizona, came to take the job in Bend in 1990.

"I was hoping we'd have some time to catch up," Morrow said. "How're you doing after your incident overseas?"

"I'm good. It's about time I return to my post."

"I was in the Navy," the older man said, "during Vietnam. We shipped out of Long Beach on the USS Eversole. My wife, Laura, got to go on a dependent's cruise off Catalina Island before we left." He laughed and added, "She loved that destroyer! Said that if we ever went on a cruise, it'd have to be a large ship like that one."

Cal smiled, took a sip of the strong coffee and said, "My dad was in Vietnam, in the Army."

"Yes, I know." Morrow's brow furrowed. "We talked about our involvement in that war many times over some beers."

"He didn't tell us much about it," Cal said.

"I think it was because we both had experienced it," Morrow said sadly.

"My sophomore year in high school was when I first came here to work. I was just sixteen."

"I remember."

"I told you that I was thinking of getting into law enforcement."

"Yep." Morrow smiled. "You were a promising candidate to becoming a great police officer."

"That's not the real reason I came here."

Both men were silent for a few seconds as the clock above the sheriff's desk ticked away. Then, Morrow said, "I think I knew that."

"I was hoping to get some information about my dad's shooting," Cal said, relieved to finally reveal the truth to this man he'd always admired.

Sheriff Morrow nodded. "I had just turned Deputy when your dad's case came in – it was my first murder."

"I wish I knew who killed him." Cal sighed and leaned forward in his seat, placing his elbows on his knees. "He never should've been up on that range alone."

"But, that's what your dad did," Morrow said. "He liked to work solo. And, being on that remote range, nobody could've heard any gunshots." Seeing the look on Cal's face, he added, "There was evidence that John fired his rifle before he died."

Cal's head came up sharply. "I never heard that! Could his killer have been hit? Dad always was a good shot."

Morrow shrugged. "I guess we'll never know."

There was another long silence, then the sheriff said, "Luther's parents have been notified."

"I can't just sit around and do nothing," Cal said as he stood and put on his cap. "I think I'll go down there to meet his parents…if that's okay with you."

"It's a free country. Just keep our evidence to yourself."

"Understood, sir."

CHAPTER 22

DRIVING THROUGH LA PINE, south of Bend, Cal looked at the Umpqua National Forest and the snowy view of the Cascade Mountain Range. He knew he had over a two-hour drive ahead of him to Klamath Falls, but he didn't mind with scenery like this.

He was looking forward to learning more information – like why Luther left his home at such a young age. He never would discuss it when they were fishing or hunting together. But, today, Cal was going to use his skills as a Recon Marine – gathering intel.

He came into the small community of Crescent, near the Gold Lake ski area on the eastern side of the Cascade Range. He used to come to Crescent Lake during summer break with his dad to fly fish. It was shaped like a crescent moon.

Realizing he was hungry, Cal pulled into the parking lot of the Bigfoot Tavern for lunch. As he walked toward the entrance, a large carved wooden statue of Bigfoot holding a mug greeted him.

Inside, the place was busy with mostly locals. All looked up as he entered, but then went back to their discussions.

He sat at the bar and ordered a Bigfoot burger and a beer. Over the bar hung a faded painting of an old stagecoach being attacked by American Indians. The conversations around him were about hunting and fishing.

"I caught an eight pound brook trout this morning," one guy said.

"Did you hear about that fellow who caught that twenty-eight pound brown trout up at Paulina Lake?" another added.

Cal enjoyed the fish stories, but kept to himself. He didn't feel like engaging in any conversation just then. His thoughts now were on hopefully finding answers to some of the questions he had about Luther in Klamath Falls. His food arrived and he ate silently.

Totally satisfied, he walked outside to his Jeep as two couples were getting off their antique Harley motorcycles. One woman got out of a sidecar. When she turned to put her helmet on the seat, she had a leather jacket with the emblem for the "Oregon Trail Chapter" of the Antique Motorcycle Club of America on the back. Cal smiled when he saw one man's T-shirt had *Old motorcycles don't leak, they mark their spot* printed on the front.

As he got into his vehicle, Cal looked back at the bike with the sidecar and was reminded of Dr. Jordan Hansen. She was an enigma that he wanted to get to know better. Their pasts were similar, but she had other mysteries that intrigued him - like the time between when she finished medical school in Nebraska to her job in San Diego. But, then, he quickly reminded himself that he wasn't interested in starting a relationship with any woman just yet.

CAL DROVE ON THE Dalles-California Highway, which began back in 1926. He passed the sign for Crater Lake and thought of how he loved the history of Oregon. When the Mt. Mazama volcano erupted thousands of years ago, the caldera and pristine lake were created.

He remembered going there in the summer with his family when he was young. They would stay in the old lodge that had been built in 1915. Cal especially liked when they would go out on the lake in a small boat to what is now called 'Wizard Island', a cinder dome left from that momentous eruption.

Now, the road continued along the border of the Upper Klamath Lake, the largest freshwater lake west of the Rocky Mountains. Suddenly, a huge swarm of the famous Klamath midge now hit his windshield as he entered the city of Klamath Falls. Those pests would appear every year at the same time, but this batch seemed a little later than most years.

Cal stopped at a gas station to clear his windshield. A husky guy wearing a baseball cap came out of the building.

"Can I help you?" he asked.

"No, thanks," Cal said as he took the squeegee from the bucket near the pump. "I've got this."

"Ah, the little green bugs got you," the man said with a laugh and sauntered back to the station.

Before he left, Cal looked at a paper on the seat next to him. He noted the address for the Klamath County Museum, where he'd arranged for a meeting with Edith Hadley, the local Historian, which he felt was a good place to start.

He drove by the Linkville Cemetery, where fall maple trees was starting to create a blanket of gold over the landscape of old and new gravestones.

Sadly, Cal was reminded of the reason for his visit.

CHAPTER 23

CAL PARKED HIS JEEP outside the museum, near where an old Weyerhaeuser train caboose sat. As he walked into the red brick building, he was surprised to see a full-sized covered wagon and display of vintage cars on the first floor. Up on a balcony, was an assortment of old washing machines.

A rock collection, next to a 1929 Ford Model A, caught his eye and he went over to the glass case. He'd been a rock hound most of his life and Central Oregon had some of the most interesting sources of agates, obsidian, and what was known as Thundereggs, which was voted Oregon's state rock back in 1965. Those rocks form in lava flows and have a non-descript outer shell. But once one was opened, an array of colorful minerals was hidden inside.

"Hello," a voice said behind him, echoing in the large open space.

He turned and saw a slender woman smiling at him. She had short dark hair and chestnut-colored eyes behind her horn-rimmed glasses. She extended her hand and said,

"I'm Amanda Gilmore. Can I help you?"

Cal shook her hand. "I'm Cal Jamison – I have an appointment with the Historian, Edith Hadley."

"I'm so sorry, but Edith had an emergency at home. A neighbor called to tell her that her cat got out. Snuffles is a rescue kitty and doesn't have front claws."

She saw the disappointed look on Cal's face and added, "I've been training with Edith for a year now – she's planning to retire next month. So, maybe we can talk in the office."

Amanda led the way to a glass cubicle in one corner of the museum. Photos of the county landscape before all of the development hung around the small room. She sat behind an antique oak desk and waited.

Cal took a seat across from her and said, "I'm here to see Luther Greeves' parents."

"But, this is a museum—" she began.

"I know. But, my grandfather told me to first talk with Edith when I arrived – they're old friends."

Amanda smiled, her high cheekbones causing her glasses to rise. "And who is your grandfather?"

"Glenn Jamison."

The young woman's eyes opened wide. "Oh, you're from THAT Jamison family. One of your ancestors helped to build the Oregon Trail."

"Yes, Callum Jamison," he said, smiling. "I was named after him."

"You are famous in all of Oregon! Well, your family is – they date back to the early eighteen-hundreds."

"Yes, I know."

There was an awkward silence for a moment. He didn't really like talking about his family that much.

She adjusted some papers on her desk, folded her hands in front of her, and cleared her throat. "You said something about Luther Greeves."

"Yes, I need to talk with his parents. But, I'd like some information first."

"I saw the news about Luther's death," she said as she took off her glasses. "I went to high school with him." She sighed heavily, then asked, "What information do you want?"

He took out a small notepad and pen from his coat pocket that he'd brought. "Can you tell me why he left when he was just a junior in high school?"

She nodded. "It was mostly because of his father."

"I learned that Luther had been arrested a few times when young." Micco was the one who'd found that bit of info, but Cal didn't mention that. "Can you tell me anything about it?"

"Well, he and Bobby Crystal were best buddies. Both were always together at rodeos and on the football team – until they were kicked out of school."

"Why?"

"Bobby was caught with drugs near the school grounds. Luther was with him when he was arrested, but the officials didn't have anything on him - other than his association with Bobby. School policy caused them both to be expelled."

"I see," he said, making a few notes. Then, he stood up and said, "Thanks for your help." He put his notepad away. "Well, I think I'd better be going."

Quickly, she stood up, grabbed her glasses and a jacket. "I want to come with you – if that's alright."

CHAPTER 24

THE CLOCK TICKED AWAY the seconds as Cal and Amanda sat on the paisley-covered couch in the Greeves' living room. A tray of tea and cookies sat on the coffee table before them. The elderly man and woman, sitting in wing-backed chairs across from them, stared at each other. Then, the gray-haired woman wiped her eyes.

Cal leaned in and rested his elbows on his knees. This was something he'd learned in the military when he needed information from a family member or a suspect on a "case" he was assigned to. It was a subservient position that seemed to put others at ease.

"I knew Luther, when he lived in Bend," Cal said.

"He was such a good boy—" Mollie Greeves began.

"That good for nothin'!" the old man roared. "I blame that boy for everything that went wrong in my life. I even lost my job at the saw mill after he and that no good Bobby Crystal got kicked out of high school. Those two boys fought all the time."

Cal looked at Amanda and saw her shake her head.

"But, he went to Bend and got that job as an auto mechanic," Mollie intervened.

"Got that girl pregnant—" Larry Greeves said.

"And he did the right thing and married her," Mollie added in Luther's defense. She looked sadly at her visitors. "We have two grandchildren that I hardly ever get to see."

"Mr. Greeves," Amanda said softly, "I knew Luther, too. I'm sure that nothing he did would have caused you to lose your job."

"You don't know nothin'!" Greeves yelled as he stood up. "Now get out of my house!"

Cal stood and said, "Thank you for your time."

Amanda touched Mrs. Greeves' shoulder. "Mollie, I am so sorry. Please let me know if there is anything I can do."

OUTSIDE, CAL TOOK A deep breath. "Wow, I see now why Luther avoided his old man."

Amanda shook her head. "Yes, Larry Greeves has always been a hothead. And, I don't think he'd been drinking yet."

"Well," Cal said, "I'd better start heading back. I've got some chores to do at my grandfather's ranch."

"I've only told you a small amount..." She looked at her watch. "I need to get home to feed my pups. Do you have time to come with me so we can talk more?"

"Absolutely."

CHAPTER 25

CAL FOLLOWED AMANDA'S GOLD Oldsmobile 88 to the east part of Klamath Falls. She parked the vintage car in front of a white 1950s house with a red roof. He'd been surprised to see the pristine condition of the vehicle.

"When my parents passed away," Amanda explained, "I inherited the house and everything inside – including the car. Dad always kept it in the garage."

A dog barked as she walked up to unlock the back door. Then, a cacophony of barking broke out when she entered the kitchen.

"Hi, Toby...Prince. Sit." Both animals obediently plopped their butts on the floor and looked up at her eagerly. She took out two small treats from a jar on the turquoise laminated countertop, leaned down and gave each of the Cavalier King Charles spaniels their snacks.

"Great dogs," Cal said as the older one came up to him to sniff his hand.

"That's Toby," she said as she removed her jacket and laid it on a chair in the kitchen. "He's been with me now for seven years."

Cal glanced around the room and saw a Westinghouse stove similar to one that Glenn had before they remodeled. His grandmother missed her old stove.

"I'm training Prince to be a Companion Dog," Amanda said as she scratched the head of the smaller dog. She straightened and asked, "Want some coffee?"

"Sure. Black."

Amanda filled an orange teapot with water from a vintage farmhouse sink and placed the pot on the stove. Cal was surprised when she took a French Press from a cabinet – the only modern device in the kitchen.

She smiled as she scooped coffee into the press and said, "I don't drink a lot of coffee, and I hate the smell of old coffee. But, I do like to make it available for guests."

He looked through the open archway into the living room. An oval coffee table was in the center. Other small tables sat against the outer walls with knickknacks and bronze statues scattered among them. A large beveled-glass mirror hung by the front door.

"I can see what you mean about inheriting everything."

Amanda came over and stood next to him. She sighed and said, "I just can't bring myself to change anything. I miss them so much."

"I live with my grandparents. They still have some of the stuff they brought from the large ranch after Glenn decided to break out on his own."

She smiled. "Families."

"Isn't Gilmore Irish?"

"Yes, Dad's ancestors were from the Ulster region of northern Ireland. I have a family tree hung upstairs."

"Tell me more about Luther," he said to get back on track.

"Well, he always seemed to have a chip on his

shoulder, but I understood why." She looked at Cal and shook her head. "His father beat him something terrible. I knew, but Luther wouldn't let me tell anyone…That's why he left."

Cal nodded. "I understand a lot more now."

After the coffee maker was heated, he watched as she put a San Francisco Bay pod.

"This company uses less non-compostable materials in their pods, which I appreciate." Amanda turned and added, "I'm also an avid gardener."

She let the coffee brew into a porcelain mug that looked like it was from an old diner. "Go on in and have a seat," she said.

Cal walked into the living room and saw an old camera laying on a side table. Then, some fossils on the table under the mirror caught his eye. He walked over to the ancient artifacts and was amazed to see two Ammonites as big as his hand, one untouched and the other sliced in half to reveal the intricate internal formation of the extinct sea snail.

Amanda joined him and handed him a mug.

"I love fossils," Cal said.

"My dad was a Geologist. He traveled all over the world on digs until I was born." She picked up a slice of ancient clear, yellow and orange stone with a dragonfly trapped inside. "He found this on the shores of the Baltic Sea and wished he'd named me after the Amber tree resin."

She sat on the long velvet, rolled-arm sofa in front of a bay window overlooking some fir trees near her driveway. Cal chose a red swivel arm chair across from the oval coffee table.

"What kind of man was Luther?" she asked. "I only knew him as a kid."

"Luther was a good man. In spite of his upbringing, he

was a kind husband and father. He had two kids: a sixteen-year-old boy, and a sweet ten-year-old girl." Cal took a sip of the dark liquid. "He was a volunteer firefighter – captain of the First Responder team and was injured in a fire last year."

Cal stopped there. He still wasn't sure that his death wasn't related somehow to that fire.

A sadness fell over Amanda's eyes. She ran her hand through her short hair and said, "I wish I had stayed in touch all these years."

He didn't know what to say after that, so he took another sip.

Finally, he asked, "What do you know about Bobby Crystal?"

"He lives alone. When his dad retired, his parents moved to Florida. After Bobby got out of jail, he went into the Army, but was discharged early for some reason."

Just then, Prince jumped up onto Amanda's lap. She laughed and stroked the silky coat as the pup looked up at her with his large round eyes. Toby, the older dog, lay content on the large dog bed next to the vintage RCA console television.

"Prince is going to live with a woman who has abuse issues. These spaniels are so affectionate and calming. They both have the red-on-white coloring. Toby has the Blenheim spot on his forehead, which is known as the 'Duchess's Thumb Print.' Only a few dogs have that mark."

"They sure are cute. And, I appreciate people who train dogs as companions."

"If I ever get married, I want to carry one of these pups instead of a flower bouquet."

Cal laughed, glad for the change in conversation. "If you do, just don't throw it like you would a bouquet."

THERE WAS A KNOCK at the door. Amanda got up and opened it. Cal saw a UPS truck parked outside.

"Kyle," she said. "What're you doing here?"

The man in the familiar brown uniform smiled playfully and said, "I have a package for you."

She took the box, missing the inuendo. "Can you stay for a cup of coffee?"

"Sure. You're the last stop on my route."

Cal smiled as he figured this guy always made Amanda his last stop so he could spend time with her. He was of medium height, with a muscular build. Another part of Cal's job in the Marines was reading people. There was something about him that Cal recognized.

Kyle walked in, but stopped when he saw Cal. "Am I intruding?"

Amanda said, "Not at all. Kyle Bevan, meet Cal Jamison. He's here about Luther."

Kyle and Cal shook hands while Amanda went into the kitchen.

"I knew Luther, too," the young man said as he sat on the couch. "It was sad to see the news about him… How well did you know Luther?"

"Well enough," Cal said. "He and I would go fly fishing together."

"He loved hunting best," Kyle said. "And the rodeo."

"Amanda and I went to see Luther's parents. His dad said something about him and another man who were always fighting."

"Yeah, that would be Bobby."

Amanda returned. Kyle took the mug of coffee from her and added, "Even though they were inseparable, those two fought over everything – girls, football, rodeos. I once saw Bobby attack Luther at a rodeo in Pendleton, claiming Luther had cheated on one of the major rides. It wasn't the first time he'd threatened to kill Luther. But, I think Bobby had a more serious reason to hate him."

"Why is that?" Cal asked.

Kyle looked away, then turned and said, "Bobby was in the Army…He always blamed Luther for somehow getting him discharged for a violation."

Cal thought for a moment. He could see the young man was holding something back.

"Do you know Bobby's address?" Cal asked.

"Yes," Kyle said, "but he's not there. I stopped to make a delivery before I came here, but no one was home."

Then, Amanda looked outside and saw two small deer come out of the stand of trees near her driveway. She said, "Awe, look at them – they're so sweet. One year I had a large buck shot by my house."

She looked at Kyle, then added, "Well, we think it was a deer. We'd just had some snow and I was out taking some pictures with my dad's Nikon F2 camera." She nodded toward the camera Cal had seen earlier. "Those cameras were used in the 50s by war correspondents during Vietnam."

Cal thought of his own dad in that war…

"She's an amazing photographer," Kyle said.

Amanda blushed. "Photography is another hobby. So, last December, I came upon what I thought was a murder scene – there was a lot of blood in the snow on my driveway—"

"She called me and I came right over," Kyle interjected.

"My neighbors were out of town, so I was glad he did."

"We only found deer prints, no human footprints, but we never found the deer."

He laughed and added, "Amanda had called for a pizza

before she went out to take her photos. The pizza guy arrived and almost wet himself seeing all that blood."

"Did it bother you?" Cal asked.

"I've seen worse."

Amanda said, "I developed that roll of film back then, but never made prints." She looked over at the old camera. "I'll have to do that someday."

Cal stood up. "Well, I'd better be heading back to Bend. It was nice meeting you both and thank you so much for your help."

He took the notepad out of his pocket, wrote down his information, then handed it to Amanda. "Here's my phone number. Please let me know if either of you have any information on Bobby."

He and Kyle shook hands and he left. As he walked to his car, Cal thought, *Yep, the guy's military.*

ON THE WAY OUT of Klamath Falls, Cal stopped at the Texaco station he'd stopped at before, this time to fill up his Jeep. He wished now that he'd flown, since now he had a few hours' drive ahead of him and he was tired.

As the same guy came out, Cal appreciated that Oregon was one of the few states that still had gas pump attendants. Other states around him had voted to have car owners pump their own gas, but he liked that his state gave jobs to people for this service. And, compared to most states, the gas was still cheaper.

"You're that fellow who was here before," the wiry man with long sandy hair and beard said.

Cal just nodded and gave him his order.

As the man pumped the gas, he said, "You're not from around here are ya?"

"How can you tell?" Cal asked the man. He noticed the

logo on his cap - a hairy dude with a Viking helmet.

The guy nodded toward the Cougar decal on Cal's windshield. "I went to Mazama here – we're Vikings!"

Cal smiled. The decal was from the previous owner, but he knew better than to get into high school football rivalry.

"Do you know Bobby Crystal?" he asked as he gave cash to the attendant.

"Yeah."

"Where can I find him?" Cal asked.

The man pushed his hat back and scratched his head. "Don't know where he is now, but I heard that he was in the Army - some kind of sharp-shooter."

CHAPTER 26

THE NEXT MORNING, CAL was exhausted. After the drive back, it had been late when he got home and everyone was in bed. He'd tossed and turned for a few hours going over everything in his mind and didn't get to sleep until three AM.

As he got dressed, he thought he'd better share the information he'd learned in Klamath Falls with Sheriff Morrow. But, before he did, he needed to talk to Micco.

Walking up the stairs to the loft above the garage, Cal called out. "Anybody home?"

"Yep," his friend answered.

Cal wasn't surprised to see a large white board sitting in the living area with his photos and notes on Luther's murder.

"You look like hell," his friend said.

"Late night. I can see you've been busy."

"I wanted to get an early start on what we have so far.

"I've got more to add." Cal posted his notes he'd made during his trip to Klamath Falls and filled Micco in with other details about Luther's death.

"It looks like that trip was worth it."

"I feel like I'm not doing my share of the work around here. Is there anything I can do?" Cal asked.

"Nah, I've got it covered. My cousin, Tocho, is coming over later to help me move the horses to another pasture."

"Thanks, man. I owe you."

Micco smiled. "And, I'll collect someday."

They stood for a long while, going over everything. Cal was reminded of when he was assigned a new mission. It had been a long while since he'd felt that surge of excitement.

"You know something?" Cal said. "This is the first time since I've been on medical leave that I feel like I have a purpose." He stopped and then asked Micco, "Are you glad you retired?"

"Absolutely, but what brought that up?" his friend asked.

Cal thought for a moment, then said, "Never mind."

"Okay then, what's next, boss?"

"I met a guy named Kyle Bevan who knew both Luther and this Bobby Crystal I told you about. Could you look into Kyle for me? He works for UPS and I'm pretty sure he has a military background."

"Sure thing."

"Also, Bobby was in the Army and received a dishonorable discharge. I need to know why," Cal said.

"Roger that."

"I'm going into town to stop by the sheriff's office, but first I want to talk with a local reporter. She may be able to help us with some research."

As Cal was about to leave, Micco said, "Oh, your brother called, summoning you for that meeting at the Jamison later today."

"Jack's going to have to wait."

CHAPTER 27

CAL ENTERED THE STARBUCKS on Wall Street in Bend and saw the older strawberry-blonde woman sitting at a table in the back. Betty Nolan waved as he went up to the counter to place his order. With so many choices to choose from, the young clerk wasn't sure what to do when he just asked for black coffee.

While he waited,, he looked around. Some of the people were locals he recognized, but there were a few tourists with exotic drinks sitting at tables outside the front door. One couple had a golden Labradoodle laying at their feet.

He went to join the woman he'd known for years. Betty was his English teacher in high school and he always knew she'd end up being a writer. She was now the leading newspaper reporter for the Bend Gazette and he wasn't surprised to see her pad of paper and pen laying on the table.

"Hey, Betty," Cal said as he sat down. "It's good to see you again."

"Cal Jamison...I wondered what happened to you. But, then, unlike your brother, you always like to keep your name out of the news."

He smiled. There wasn't much that happened around the area that Betty didn't know.

She took a sip of her drink, which had 'Cappuccino' written on the paper cup. Then, she said, "So, what can I do for you? You said on the phone that this was important."

"Well, I'm here about Luther Greeves."

She nodded sadly. "We're going to miss him."

"You probably remember that fire at Hawk Plastics about a year ago – the one that killed one of Bend's firemen."

Betty looked down for a moment, then back up into Cal's dark eyes. "Yes, I knew Jeremy Lockhart. He was a great kid."

"I'd like you to do some research on that for me. I'm also interested in whatever you can find on Luther." He didn't share yet that he was investigating Luther's death.

"Wasn't he injured in that same fire?"

Cal looked around and was glad to see the table nearest them was empty. He leaned in and softly said, "The case was determined as 'Unknown Causes.' I'm just wondering if that fire wasn't arson."

Betty's eyes widened. "Do you think Luther's death and the first fire are somehow related?"

Cal nodded his head. Of course, she'd know about Luther's recent death – he just wasn't sure how much she knew.

She made some notes on her pad, excited to be able to do some real research for a change - with the possibility of a juicy story in the end. Lately, most of her pieces were about weddings and funerals.

"See if you can find info on fire calls Luther was on for the past year or so. He was still suffering from amnesia and couldn't remember much about the first fire." He looked around again and added, "Please keep this under your hat."

Betty smiled. "I'm on it!"

CAL HAD PARKED HIS Jeep a block from Starbucks. As he walked down the main street through town, he thought of how Betty always liked a good mystery for her stories. She mostly called them 'stories' – not 'articles' for the newspaper. Once, she'd told him that her granddaughter asked if her job was to make up stories. But, Cal knew that Betty liked to get her facts straight on anything she wrote.

As he came to the Raven Gallery window, he stopped, surprised to see Mary, Jamie's sister, inside. She was talking with an older couple. He shook his head when he saw the odd colors she wore - a purple leather jacket over a chartreuse sweater and yellow slacks.

He decided to go in.

When Mary looked his way, he smiled and continued around the gallery. Paintings of the Northwest hung on the walls. A few bronze statues sat on pedestals – one in particular of a Bald Eagle in flight caught his eye. He continued to the back of the room and in one corner was an intricately designed, wooden pendulum clock. He was mesmerized by the inner workings and didn't hear the soft footsteps behind him.

"Hello, Cal," Mary said.

He turned and was stunned by her beauty. Her hair was pulled up in back and her green eyes shone in the overhead canned lighting. He took a deep breath and said, "Hi...I hadn't been in here for some time and thought I'd stop by." He knew he was lying, because he was hoping to find a way to see her again.

"Is there anything I can help you with?"

"Are you working here?"

She nodded and said, "I'm just helping a friend of Jamie's out for a little while."

Looking around, he realized they were alone and his palms were sweating. He never got like that. Unsure why he let her get under his skin, he took a deep breath and said, "I was hoping…you knew where Jamie was. I tried to call her this morning, but there was no answer."

"She and the kids took a few days to go up to Paulina Lake."

"So, they're doing okay?"

"Yes, so far. Jamie wants to get back to work – she doesn't want to be alone at the house when the kids go back to school."

He looked around the room, stalling to calm down. "Do you have any of your art here?"

"No, but I'm inspired by some of the works of these local artists. I was excited to see there was a class in Prineville that use local materials for painting, but they were full right now."

Cal could hear the animation in her voice and had seen that same light in his grandmother's eyes when she was working on her own art. He also noted Mary's disappointment.

"My grandmother is an artist," he offered. "She's also a Northern Paiute Indian. Maybe you and she could meet up some time to talk."

"I'd love that!"

He found a gallery card, wrote down Winnie's number on the back, and handed it to her.

"Thank you so much." She looked down at her watch

and said, "I'm sorry, but I have another client coming in soon."

"That's okay, I have somewhere I need to be."

CAL LEFT THE BUILDING. *What the hell was that all about?* he asked himself silently. He didn't let women get close to him for good reason. If he'd been on a mission, he'd probably be dead right now.

Just as he got into his Jeep, he got a call. Looking down at the screen on his cell phone, he frowned. It was his eldest brother. Usually, he ignored Jack's calls because he always seemed to rant about something only important to himself, but this time Cal decided to answer it.

"What's up, Jack?" he said, smiling as he goaded his brother.

"You know what the hell is up," the voice on the other end said. "Why aren't you here at the ranch?"

"I've been busy."

"You're retired now – what the hell do you have to do?"

"I'm on medical leave – not retired."

"I've got big investors coming today. We're looking to make some changes and I need you here—"

"Jack, you haven't needed me at the homestead in years."

There was silence on the other end. The two brothers had been quarreling for a long time – since their father died.

Then, Jack said, "Mom wants you here."

Cal took a deep breath and slowly let it out before he answered. "I just can't get there now."

Another silence. Then, Cal quickly added, "I've got another call coming in. Talk to you later."

He hung up and sat there for a moment, pissed that his brother hadn't once asked how their grandfather was doing.

CHAPTER 28

AS CAL ENTERED THE sheriff's office, Andy came out of the break room carrying a coffee mug. He was the only one in the office.

"Hey, Cal," Andy asked. "What brings you in here today?"

"Got any more of that coffee?" he asked.

"Sure, help yourself."

Cal went back to the familiar room. He sighed as he looked over the wanted posters on the board above the stained coffee pot. Some faces he recognized, but there were many others he didn't know. Realizing he'd had enough coffee, he went to the vending machine and got a bottle of water. Then, he joined his friend.

Cal sat on the chair at the end of Andy's desk. "We've known each other since we were kids playing football. I was a quarterback and you were my wide receiver. Here we are now, me still single and you married with three kids."

Andy laughed. "We've been through a lot since we were kids. How're you doing?"

Cal shrugged, then regretted it. "Okay – for now. Not sure where I'm going next."

"You don't mean getting out of the military…"

"Not sure."

They were both silent for a moment.

In football, Cal could always depend on Andy on the field. The two of them made a great team, anticipating what the other needed most of the time. But, right now, Cal wasn't even sure what the next play was in his life.

Andy cleared his throat. "The other day, when I went to the State Police lab, Steve Johns talked to me about possibly joining their detective team."

"That's awesome!" Cal said excitedly. "You've been a detective here for six years now. I always thought you were too good for this job."

"Thanks, man. Your confidence in me will help making my decision easier."

Andy opened a file on his desk and fanned out some photos of the crime scene. "We've gone over the evidence, but the only thing we found so far were the tire tracks leading from Luther's camp to where the fire was - possibly an SUV. That could be anyone out there hunting."

"Sheriff said you were working on the tire castings."

Andy looked at his friend and smiled. "Nothing gets by you." He pulled out one photo and pointed. "The tracks were made by a Les Schwab Back Country Touring H/T tire – like most tires around here."

"Damn," Cal said. "I was hoping for something more conclusive."

"Me, too."

Cal looked around the empty room. "You could lose your job if you get caught showing me these."

"I know," Andy said, "but I thought you might see something we've missed."

After quickly scanning the other photos, Cal said, "When I first arrived, I noticed everything around the campsite was swiped clean, no foot tracks. We're dealing with a professional here. But the tire tracks you found explain finding Luther's body in a burning bush a hundred yards away - especially if he was still alive…"

"I agree." Andy said, then looked down at Luther's file. "Those papers at the campsite were interesting, That fire last year turned out to be an accident, but Luther just wouldn't let it go. He even stole the investigator's report from the firehouse."

"I think Luther always believed it was arson. Maybe his death is connected to it."

A SQUAD CAR PULLED up out front and Andy quickly closed the file and put it in a drawer. After a moment, Sheriff Morrow and Deputy Rupert Bateman walked in.

Morrow saw Cal and said, "What the hell are you doing here again, Jamison?"

"I was in Klamath Falls yesterday—" Cal began.

"So?" Bateman interrupted. "I don't like the way you keep sticking your nose into police business."

Andy sat at his desk and waited.

Cal stood up and said, "I talked with Luther's parents. His dad is a piece of work."

"Yep," Andy added, glad Cal had changed the subject. "I heard he's a mean drunk and that's why Luther left before he finished high school."

Cal nodded. "I also met the historian there, Amanda Gilmore, and her friend, Kyle Bevan, who drives a UPS truck. They both went to school with Luther."

"What's that got to do with this case?" Bateman asked gruffly, his arms folded across his broad chest.

114

Standing with his back to Bateman, Cal said to the sheriff, "I learned something interesting – Luther and a guy named Bobby Crystal always fought. They both got in trouble in high school and Crystal blames Luther for his dishonorable discharge from the Army. He was even heard to threaten Luther's life a few times."

"There's a couple good reasons to talk with him," Morrow said.

"And, he was a sniper," Cal added.

The men looked at each other for a moment. Then, Morrow said, "Bateman, get an ATL out on this guy."

Cal knew that was an 'Attempt To Locate' code.

A beep came from the FAX machine across the room. Andy went to pick it up and read the contents.

Cal was about to continue, but stopped. He could tell by the look on his friend's face that something was wrong. "What's up?" he asked.

Looking out the window, Andy said, "This is from Dr. Hansen, the ME." He took a deep breath, looked back at Cal and the others and added, "She finished Luther's autopsy."

"And?" the sheriff asked.

Andy relayed the medical examiner's info about the knife tip to the sheriff. "She confirmed that Luther was severely tortured with a knife."

Cal added, "We're probably looking for someone with military experience."

"What do you mean 'we?'" Bateman said sharply. "You don't work here, remember?"

"That's enough, Rupert," Morrow said.

"I just wonder if they got what information they wanted…" Cal said, then picked up his water bottle to take a sip. He wanted to get the foul taste out of his mouth that seemed to rise anytime he came near Bateman.

Andy took a deep breath, looked at his friend and added, "The Post-Mortem Report also says that, based on the carbon monoxide test, the Cause of Death was Asphyxia due to smoke inhalation."

"Jesus," Morrow said.

Cal choked on his water. He wiped his mouth with the back of his hand as anger rose inside of him. He said softly, "You mean Luther was still alive when he was put on that pyre?"

Sadly, Andy could only nod his head.

The sheriff took the report from Andy. After a few moments, he looked up and said, "She doesn't know yet when the body will be released."

CHAPTER 29

PULLING UP TO THE house at the Double J, Cal sat in his Jeep for a while, chilled to the bone. He squeezed his eyes tight, trying to black out some of the images running through his mind of what Luther must have suffered... The one thing he never would understood was the evil that drives some people. This was one of the few times he wished he could start his life all over again.

The only saving grace was that Luther had probably been unconscious by the time his body was torched. But then, his anger rose again and Cal knew he had to work it off before he went inside the house.

He marched to the stable and saw the stalls needed mucking. Thankful to finally be doing something physical, he put on his gloves and let the horses out into their outside runs. With each pitchfork full of sullied straw, his shoulder and back ached, but he ignored the pain.

In his mind, he relived some of the horrors he'd seen during his missions across the globe and his own attack when he was injured. His MARSOC team was in the

Helmand Province of Afghanistan, near the town of Sangin, one of the largest opium-producing regions in the world. On one training mission, they took heavy sniper fire and one of his men stepped on an IED near him…

Bravo whinnied and Cal became aware of his surroundings. He stopped and took a deep breath as he saw that he was no longer on patrol in the arid desert across the globe.

Cal knew the horses could sense his angry mood, so he sat down on a bale of hay. He never cried, but now he wish he could - for the horror he knew Luther had endured and for the loss of his men in Afghanistan. He leaned back against the stall, looking skyward for some answers. But, once again, he felt only frustration, knowing that there was nothing he could have done to prevent any of it.

GLENN WALKED INTO THE barn and stood by the door, watching his grandson. This wasn't the first time he'd seen Cal wrestling with his demons.

"You okay, son?" the older man asked.

With a heavy sigh, Cal got up, removed his gloves and walked to his grandfather.

"Yeah, just got some bad news today. Got any coffee?"

"I've got something stronger, if you want…"

"Let me get the horses back in and fed and I'll be in."

"I'll give you a hand."

The two men worked side by side just as they had done for years when Cal was a young boy. Cal took the filled wheel barrow to the back of the barn and returned for another load. But, this time was different. They didn't chat about the weather or livestock, not like they used to. They worked in silence.

IT WAS DARK WHEN the two men entered the house and removed their boots at the door. The smell of hot oil was in the air.

Winnie came out of the kitchen, wiping her hands on a small white towel and said, "You are just in time. I am about to fry some fish for dinner." She stopped when she saw her grandson's face and looked at her husband.

Cal hugged his small grandmother. "I love you, Winnie." Then he remembered Mary's business card and gave it to her. "You may get a call from a woman named Mary. She's Jamie Creswell's sister and is an artist, like you."

"Is she pretty?" Winnie asked, trying to lighten the mood.

He just smiled.

"Go on into the den, son," Glenn said. He gently touched Winnie's cheek and winked to let her know he would take care of their grandson. "Give us a few minutes before starting the fish, okay?"

Winnie kissed her husband and returned to the kitchen.

Glenn joined Cal and went to the long bar he'd bought from a friend in Prineville. He poured two fingers of a bottle of twenty-one-year-old Oban single malt Scotch whiskey.

Cal was stretched out on the long couch. He was exhausted and distracted himself by looking around the room. Thinking that the Mission-style furniture worked well with the log walls of the building helped him to breathe easier.

A fire burned in the large fireplace with 'Jamison' carved in a wide rock above the flames. Over the mantel was Cal's dad's rifle, mounted under the family Coat of

Arms containing three anchors and a ship under sail. He was thankful this was his home.

"You know, Cal, ever since me birthday, I only bring out the Oban on special occasions," Glenn said as he handed Cal a glass and sat his large frame down in the tall armchair with the red leather seat. "I be grateful for your generous gift."

Cal raised his glass, said "*Sláinte*" in the Gaelic toast Glenn always used, and took a sip. The smoky, salty flavor hit his senses.

"Ah," Glenn sighed. "A taste of home. Those lowland Scotches are too peaty and smoky for me taste."

Cal noticed that once in a while the older man would slip into a bit of the Scottish dialect that he'd heard from his ancestors. It was usually brought on by good whiskey. Cal remembered the stories Glenn told him of visiting the Oban distillery on the northwest coast of the Scottish Highlands years ago when he and his father, Clyde, decided to go back to see where their family had hailed from. Cal's great grandfather died a few years after that trip.

"You be havin' a few rough days," his grandfather said after a bit.

Cal only nodded, reality flooding back. He took another sip of the warming liquid. Eventually, he began to feel the life returning to his body. He then told his grandfather about Luther.

"I wish to hell he'd taken me hunting with him…" Cal said and took another sip.

"There's nothin' you could've done. You know how he liked to go it alone – he'd been doing that fer years."

Cal nodded again.

Glenn cleared his throat and said, "Our poker group met last night, and me buddy, Gordon Lockhart, was there. He said somethin' about Luther looking into a fire he'd been involved in…said that young man was like a dog with a bone."

That made Cal smile. "Yes, he was. I think he was looking into an arson case."

"If it was that plastics building fire, I'm not surprised. That owner was probably looking for an insurance payout."

Cal was reminded of Jack's main interest in big money versus keeping the family homestead's heritage. He tried to tamp down the pent-up emotions that always stirred in him – he'd had enough turmoil for one day.

"Cal, honey," Winnie called from the kitchen. "Can I make up a plate for you?"

"I'm sorry, Winnie, but I'm just not hungry right now." He saw the look on her face as he stood up and added, "But, I hope there'll be some waffles for breakfast."

He finished his Scotch and said, "I gotta get some rest."

As he walked by his grandfather, Cal gently placed his hand on Glenn's shoulder. "Thanks…I'm so grateful."

CHAPTER 30

BACK IN KLAMATH FALLS, it was late when Amanda got back to her darkroom. She was going over the prints she'd made earlier from that roll of film she talked about with Cal.

As she laid each one out on the table, she thought of that day. It had been early dawn when she'd looked out the window and saw something was wrong. Her father's camera was loaded with HP-5, a fast film, which was perfect for the low-lit time of day. The Nikon was a 25th Anniversary F2A camera. Only a few thousand were made and it was one of her treasures.

The images stared back at her in black and white – the dark stain on the white snow where that deer had lost its life. Something, at the edge of two prints caught her eye. She grabbed a magnifier and leaned over to get a closer look. Then, she decided to enlarge them.

She turned on the amber light, prepped the chemicals and went over to the old Beseler 23C Enlarger and felt as if her father was there watching her. She raised the head of the machine as high as it would go, which would give a sixteen-times enlargement of the original negative. She moved the easel over to capture the section she wanted. Refocusing, she made the new print.

As she prepared everything, she thought of watching her dad in the darkroom. Like Ansel Adams, he preferred black and white film to digital, and she still had some of his equipment. A few of his photos she had framed, but he never thought his work was good enough.

When finished processing all the images, she viewed the dry prints. In the left corner of each print there was a shadow. With her magnifier, she could just make out the shape of a person under the fir trees at the edge of her property. This time, she saw that it was a large man with his face turned back toward her. Even though the features were blurry, there was a familiar logo on the cap he was wearing.

Suddenly, Amanda grabbed her cell phone.

CHAPTER 31

CAL GASPED FOR AIR as he awoke, fighting as if he was buried alive. The sheets were tightly twisted around his body from his tossing and turning. This wasn't the first time he'd relived that blast in Afghanistan – and it wouldn't be the last. He always believed that intel of their mission had somehow been leaked to the enemy, but he could never prove it.

He got up, stretched his sore muscles and showered, trying to forget everything. Then, with the hot water running down his face, he wondered if the nightmare had been triggered by the news of Luther's death.

As he was getting dressed, he started to take out a clean shirt from his dresser, but stopped with his hand in midair.

A black case laid off to one side in the drawer. Cal sighed and slowly opened it. He ran a finger over the Purple Heart Medal he'd received the previous year. Every day since that mission he never forgot the two men he'd lost. They were his team, his friends. He always felt the men he served with deserved this medal more than he did.

Closing the box, he looked at his cell phone. There was a missed call from Amanda and three from his brother, Jack. He looked at his watch and decided to call Amanda later...

He deleted Jack's messages.

SNEAKING OUT OF THE house in the early light, Cal climbed the stairs to Micco's flat, knowing his friend was always up before dawn.

Leaning against the door, he found a large brown envelope. He picked it up, knocked and went in.

"I hope to god you've got some coffee," Cal said as he entered.

"Always." Micco was busy typing on his laptop that sat on the desk near a larger computer screen.

Cal saw that his friend was wearing the same clothes as the day before and he hadn't shaved. "You been up all night?" he asked.

"I was on a role," Micco said, rubbing his chin.

Cal poured the dark roast coffee into a mug with the U.S. Marine Emblem on one side. He remembered his friend had brought the souvenir back from their basic training in San Diego. He turned and asked, "Can I get you some?"

His friend raised one hand and smiled when it shook. "I think I've had enough."

Cal laughed as he walked over to the desk and laid the envelope down. He saw on the computer screen a search database with Holt Construction Company listed. He smiled and said, "We're on the same track. I was hoping to get more information on Jerry Holt."

"Figured as much, considering some of the notes Luther had made." Micco printed the page. "I found some old fire cases around here – mostly industrial sites. The cases were never solved or they closed quickly. My guess is they involved possible insurance fraud, but I'm still checking."

Cal shook his head. "When DO you sleep?"

Micco grinned. "Bat naps."

"Maybe we could go for a run later to burn off some of that caffeine."

"Possibly, after I get some sleep."

"Good. I'll see if I can get an appointment with Holt later today." Cal went over to the printer, picked up the page Micco had printed and added it to the white board. "Did you find anything else about Robert Crystal?"

"Bobby seems to be a hothead, arrested a few times for public disturbance, disorderly conduct and assault. Most of them had alcohol involved. I did find the record where he was dishonorably discharged from the Army." Micco gave Cal the details.

"How'd you get that?"

Micco only smiled.

They both knew what Micco was capable of – especially with his cyber training in the service.

"Just don't get caught," Cal cautioned. He walked to Micco's desk and said, "I've got more news – about Luther."

After he'd told Micco about the MEs report, they both were quiet for some time – each in his own way honoring Luther's life. Micco had also been in the rodeo circuit before joining the Marines.

"What's this?" Micco asked, as he picked up the envelope. Looking at the label, he handed it to Cal. "It's for you – special delivery."

Cal saw the return address. "This is from Amanda Gilmore, the girl I met in Klamath Falls. She called me last night, but I missed it." He didn't talk about his nightmare.

Micco smiled, trying to lighten the mood in the room. "Is she becoming your new girlfriend?"

Cal sighed and opened the package. "When do I have time for that?" He spread out the photos on one side of Micco's desk, then leaned over and read Amanda's note that said: *These are from that 'murder' scene at my house last December that we talked about.*

"Wow," Micco said, "these images are good. What murder scene is she talking about?"

"She thinks this was when someone shot a deer right there in town. Yes, she really knows what she's doing—" He stopped at one image.

Micco looked up at Cal. "What?"

"Is this man wearing camo carrying a sniper rifle with a suppressor?"

"Yep," Micco said, then pulled out a magnifying glass from a drawer. "Can you make out the logo on his hat?"

They looked together and Cal stood up. "I've seen that before. It's the Vikings – a local high school team. After I left Amanda's, I met a guy at a gas station wearing that same hat."

"Could it be our Bobby Crystal?"

Cal thought for a moment, taking a couple of sips of coffee. "I don't know, but then, that guy at the station did tell me Crystal was a sharp-shooter…"

He set his cup down and made copies of the images on Micco's printer. Looking at the clock on the wall, he knew it was too early to go into town. "I'll take these to the sheriff's office when they open."

"Need anything else?" Micco asked.

"Later, after you get some sleep, would you go back into that government website and find out more about Luther's service record?"

His friend smiled and nodded. "That was next on my list." Then, Micco looked up at Cal with a funny look on his face.

"What's wrong with you?" Cal asked.

"I can't feel my butt."

CHAPTER 32

OUTSIDE, CAL WAS SURPRISED to see Mary drive up in a blue BMW. He quickly put the photos in his Jeep and walked over to her.

"Nice car," he said as she stepped out.

"I got a free upgrade at the Redmond airport."

The sun caught her hair, which shimmered in the morning light. She wore black slacks and a yellow sweater. Around her neck was a scarf with a large geometric design of red, black, blue and purple.

"What're you doing here?" he asked, kicking himself for being so blunt.

"Winnie invited me for breakfast – so we could talk about art."

"Ah, then I'll escort you in."

As they walked towards the log house, she stopped and looked around at the buildings and the view. "This is beautiful!" she sighed.

"Welcome to the Double J."

CAL OPENED THE DOOR and called out, "Hello, it's only me…and Mary."

He hated that he felt so awkward around this woman he hardly knew. But then, most beautiful women made him a little nervous.

"Mary," Winnie cried out as she walked out of the kitchen. "I'm so glad you came." She embraced the younger woman as if she'd known her all her life, which surprised Mary.

"She's a hugger," Cal said with a smile.

"It's so good to meet you," Mary said and they followed Winnie back into the warm kitchen.

"Where's Glenn?" Cal asked.

"He's already out checking his cattle."

Cal was glad to see that his grandmother had made her famous cinnamon and sugar frybread, a recipe she'd learned to make from her grandmother. He grabbed one and said, "I'll just go ride out and give him a hand."

"Wait until after you've eaten," Winnie said sternly. "I brewed fresh coffee."

She poured him a cup. Reluctantly, he sat down and ate.

Mary asked Winnie, "Cal tells me that you like to paint, as well."

"Come, I will show you."

Winnie led the way to a large north-facing room at the back of the house. On one wall was one of her paintings of their log home in a winter landscape. Small twigs had been used for the bare tree limbs and tiny tips of pine trees represented a forest.

"Wow, this is amazing!" Mary exclaimed. "Do you have any of your work in a gallery?"

Winnie looked down shyly, then said, "I never sold any, but always gave them as gifts to friends and family. I put love into my art – I can't seem to put a price on that."

Mary turned and said, "I'm working temporarily at a gallery in town. Maybe I could talk to the owner…if that's okay with you." She realized she didn't know Winnie that well and now felt embarrassed at being too ambitious.

Winnie just smiled. Then, she walked over to a painting of an older woman carrying grass reeds. The reeds were real. "This was my grandmother," she said proudly. "She taught me to use primitive materials I find in nature."

"Yes, these are three-dimensional pieces. Very rare. When Cal told me about your work, I knew I wanted to meet you. I want to learn how to use the soils and materials as pigments for my oils."

"Then, maybe you and I could someday take a trip out into the hills and I will teach you. You will have to drive, though. I don't know how."

The two women walked back toward the kitchen. Winnie looked at Cal and said, "Why don't you take Mary out to see the horses before you go out to find Glenn?"

"I'd love that," Mary said. "I'll go get my camera from my car."

After Mary left, Winnie put her hand on her grandson's arm.

"Glenn told me what happened to your friend," she said softly. "I understand now what you have been going through. I'm so sorry."

"Thank you," he said, patting her hand.

"In my culture, death is a part of life. But, a violent death like Luther's is a life unfinished."

THE SUN WAS HIGHER when Cal went outside.

"Wait a minute," Mary said as she fired off some quick shots of the ranch, then they walked toward the stable.

"Winnie is astonishing," Mary said after a bit.

"Yes she is."

When they entered the large building, she said, "Ah, I love the smell of fresh hay. I miss riding. It's been so long, and there's not very many stables in Seattle."

"I don't get to ride as often as I used to."

"Why not?"

He only said, "It's complicated." Then, he brought Bravo out of his stall to saddle him.

"What a beautiful animal," she said as she walked up and held her hand to the horse's soft muzzle. "What's his name?"

"I call him Bravo. His registered name is Valiente, which means 'Bravo' in Spanish."

"He's a Kiger Mustang, right?"

"Yes," he said in surprise. "How do you know that?"

"I grew up here - until I was fourteen. My parents took me and Jamie to the Steens Mountain once. My first photos were of the Mustangs there."

After Cal groomed the horse, he set the blanket in place and hoisted the old Western saddle up onto the tall back.

"These horses weren't discovered until 1977, during a roundup near Frenchglen, Oregon." He finished tightening the cinch strap and dropped the stirrup back into place. Then, he added, "Glenn has a small herd now for breeding."

"I read about the adoption program for them when I went there."

Cal patted Bravo's neck. "Kiger mustangs were originally bred from Spanish horses brought here in the seventeenth century. That's why I felt this guy should be given a Spanish name."

"That's very interesting. Do you mind if I take a few photos?"

"Nope."

When he finished putting on the bridle, he looked up. Just then, Mary snapped another shot.

Suddenly, he felt he needed to get away from this woman. "Well, I've gotta head out," he said as he led Bravo out of the stable and got up into the saddle.

"Thank you," she said with a smile. "This has been a great opportunity today." She saluted him with one hand and said, "I'll see you later, cowboy."

CHAPTER 33

RIDING OUT ON THE range, Cal never got tired of the view, but by then, some clouds had started to roll in. He could smell rain coming.

There were few houses near this area, mostly acres of rolling pastureland. Across the road, an old chimney was all that was left of an old homestead.

Regina Dixon, from a neighboring ranch, honked as she drove by and Cal waved. She was a widow who was always trying to get Cal to come over for dinner whenever he was home on leave. Regina's brother, Clark, was one of the firefighters that had worked Luther's crime scene.

In the distance, Cal saw Glenn standing next to his old '57 Dodge pickup under a small grove of quaking Aspen. He was watching his Belties, as the Galloway cattle were sometimes called, as they grazed in a pasture of native mixed grasses. Odie, the shepherd, sat at his feet.

The Kiger mustang heard were in the fenced area to the west. One horse whinnied and Bravo answered. Cal gently nudged the horse's sides and they rode on.

"Good morning," Cal said to his grandfather as he dismounted next to the old truck. Odie ran up, waiting for a scratch.

"Hello," Glenn said. "What a glorious morning it is."

"Agreed."

"Rain's coming."

"I thought so, too," Cal said.

The two men stood together in silence for a long while as the clouds rolled in.

"You okay?" Glenn finally asked.

"Yes...I'm going into town in a bit. Is there anything I can do here to help you first?"

"Nay, I'm just enjoying being out of the house. There's not much to do now for the herds. The summer pastures are greening up with the fall rains and these cattle are perfect for this region. They'll be starting their heavier coats again. But, we still have time to get ready for winter..."

"Micco and I are here to take care of all that."

"I appreciate it. Before long, we'll need to get our hay and alfalfa supplies taken care of. And, get some mineral salt blocks..."

"We've got this," Cal assured his grandfather. He looked at the older man. "There's something I've wanted to ask you."

"What's that?"

"Why did you leave the Jamison? I know my reasons."

Glenn looked at Cal and said, "It was my father deciding to sell off some of the original homestead in 1992."

"That's the year I went into the Marines."

"Yes. It was shortly after that I learned what he had planned. That's what started the rift. I asked to be bought out so I could build my own ranch and run it as I see fit. Your brother, Jack, is a lot like my father."

They sat in silence again, each with their own pasts that had changed their lives.

Then, Glenn said sadly, "I've lost both my sons. Your father, John - you know about. Malcolm, his twin brother, was killed in Vietnam. I also lost my older brothers in World War II when I was only twelve years old."

Cal stood silently, thinking of his own losses because of wars across the world.

"That kind of loss changes a man," Glenn continued. "Life is too precious for bickering... So, I've been thinking - maybe it's time we try to make amends."

"I'm not sure Jack would agree. He's pretty set in his ways and has swayed Mom toward his plans for the big ranch - even talked about some investors the other day for some new scheme he's working on. I can see him turning the place into some kind of resort."

"Hmm."

Then, Glenn slapped his hands together and said, "Well, I best be getting back to Winnie. Come on, Odie." He opened the truck door and waited for the dog to jump in. Then, he used the side step to get in. "See you back at the ranch house," he said and drove off.

FOR THE NEXT FEW minutes, Cal stood, enjoying the solitude. *If only this peace could stay longer*, he thought. The last time he could remember feeling this calm was walking on the beach in San Diego with his mother after his Basic Training graduation. That was the last time he'd spent any quality time with her.

Nina Jamison was a strong, independent woman. She and Cal's father had met at a barn dance, the same year

John returned home from Vietnam. Shortly after, they'd married and Cal was born the following year.

The sound of machinery brought Cal back to the present. He saw a farmer gathering hay bales in a nearby field. Cecile Mathews was Glenn's neighbor who worked one of the alfalfa fields, who was also their supplier. Cal was thankful his grandfather had chosen years ago to let Cecile take care of that side of the business.

Visions of Mary popped into his head, making him wonder how his life would be different if he allowed himself to get close to a woman. But, then one previous mission had made that decision for him.

Cal's phone rang as it started to rain. He looked at the screen and answered the call. "Hey, Andy, I was about to come see you."

"I thought you'd want to know," his friend said excitedly on the other end. "We found Bobby Crystal."

CHAPTER 34

WHEN CAL ARRIVED AT the sheriff's office, he was surprised to find the place wasn't buzzing with activity. His friend, Andy, was the only one there.

"Where is everybody?" Cal asked as he sat down.

"Bateman and the sheriff are bringing Bobby in now."

"Why aren't you in on this arrest?"

"Bateman's been brown-nosing the sheriff lately." Andy sipped his coffee. "I decided to let him have this one."

"You're such a nice guy," Cal said with a smile.

"Before coming in this morning, I talked with the cook at the Brother's Café."

"I love Grumpy," Cal said.

The detective nodded. "He told me he remembered a guy in a black SUV who stopped and asked about Luther the day before we found him."

Cal thought back to his talk with Grumpy. That man was probably Luther's killer.

Andy continued. "Those tire tracks I found at the scene

were from an SUV, and one was just reported parked outside a motel near Bellevue Crossing off Route 20. That's how we found Bobby."

Cal gave Andy the envelope with Amanda's original photos. "I just got these from that woman in Klamath I told you about – Amanda Gilmore. She took these last December when a deer was killed near her house. I think you'll find them interesting."

Andy pulled out the images. His eyes widened as he said, "Is that a—"

"Yep, a rifle with a suppressor. Did you find anything on Bobby's military background?" Cal asked, even though he already knew the answer.

"Yes, he was discharged for Aggravated Assault, just as he was finishing sniper's training. The incident was at the same base where Luther was an Army Sergeant. Bobby shot at Luther and missed."

Just then, Morrow and Bateman walked in with a tall, skinny guy in handcuffs. Bateman was carrying a rifle with a scope.

Cal smiled when he saw the familiar cap like the guy wore at the Klamath Falls gas station. Maybe Bobby was Amanda's deer hunter.

"Rupert," Morrow said to his deputy, "get that rifle to the State Police for ballistics."

Leaning over, Cal softly said to Andy, "Can I watch while he's being questioned?"

Andy nodded and smiled. "Just don't get too excited and yell at the sheriff through the glass, like you did the last time."

Cal only smiled.

BEHIND THE TWO-WAY mirror, Cal and Andy looked into the interrogation room. Bobby sat handcuffed across a table from Sheriff Morrow.

"Your name is Robert Crystal, right?" Morrow asked for the recording as he opened a file.

"Bobby."

"OK, Bobby, you've been brought in to answer a few questions about the death of Luther Greeves—"

"Huh?" Bobby asked as he sat taller in his chair.

"For the record, you were found in a room at the Red Wing Motel on the outskirts of Bend - with a sniper rifle."

"Yeah, so?"

Morrow looked at the file. "I have statements from witnesses that heard you threaten Luther at the Sisters Rodeo last June. And, now, Luther is dead."

Bobby went silent.

"We have a receipt found in Luther's pocket for a Seven Eleven that's next to the Red Wing Motel."

"Luther came to see me...before he went hunting."

"Why did he come to your motel?" Morrow asked.

"I don't know. He was talking gibberish about past mistakes." Bobby pounded on the table angrily and added, "That asshole just wanted to show off his Bull-Riding Championship trophy. I should've won that damned buckle!"

"You drive a black SUV," the sheriff added. "Reports show an SUV was at the crime scene, near China Hat—"

"That wasn't mine!"

"You're looking like our main suspect."

"But I didn't do it!"

Morrow continued. "Luther was tortured and his body was put on a bonfire."

Bobby leaned back in his chair and smiled. "I used to build the bonfires for homecoming. It was something to see – we called it a fire of bones."

Behind the glass, Cal said, "He's not helping his case, is he?"

Andy shook his head.

Cal saw Bateman was now looking into the interrogation room from a window on the door.

For a few moments, Morrow just stared at his suspect. Cal knew that stare and smiled as he watched Bobby fidget in his seat. The sheriff was good at his job.

Morrow again shuffled through the papers on the table. "There was evidence at the crime scene that a sniper was present."

Bobby shuffled in his seat, but didn't say anything.

"You went to sniper training in the Army, correct?"

Bobby nodded.

"And, you received a Dishonorable Discharge for attempting to assault Luther Greeves at Fort Benning with a deadly weapon – a rifle."

Bobby just smiled.

Morrow stood up. "Robert Crystal, I'm arresting you on the suspicion of murdering Luther Greeves—"

Suddenly, Bobby got up and lunged for the sheriff, slamming him into the glass where Andy and Cal stood. Before they could move, Bateman ran into the room and got Bobby in a headlock, stopping the attack.

Morrow looked at the glass and said, "Add 'Assaulting a Public Safety Officer' to that charge."

Later, in the bullpen, Morrow was brushing off his uniform. "That son-of-a-bitch tore my shirt pocket. But, I think we have a closed case here."

Bateman said, "I like an open and shut case. I'll call the pretty ME and tell her she can release the body."

Andy and Cal looked at each other. Something didn't fit right for Cal, but he couldn't put his finger on it.

OUTSIDE, CAL WAS IN his Jeep. He called Amanda's number.

When she answered, he said, "Hi, Amanda, this is Cal Jamison. I wanted to let you know they found Bobby Crystal at a motel here in Bend. He's been arrested for Luther's murder."

"Oh, no. I can't believe it!"

"They have evidence that's pretty tight on him."

"I know he and Luther had their issues. But, I just can't see Bobby doing this."

"His discharge from the military was the turning point."

"I'm so sorry to hear this… By the way. did Kyle tell you he was also in the Army? He doesn't talk about it much."

CHAPTER 35

LUTHER'S FUNERAL WAS WELL attended. Many of his friends from the rodeo circuit and firefighters were there, as well as a few of his work buddies. Greenwood Cemetery was located near Pilot Butte. It was more like a maintained park with willows and various pine trees, except for the dotted headstones of the past and present.

Cal knew that the plot Luther was to be buried in was purchased by Jamie's parents in the seventies. After the Creswells moved to New York, they deeded their plots to Jamie and Luther. Even though Luther had lived in Klamath Falls before moving here, this was where he now belonged.

Andy Shaw joined Cal and Micco where they stood off to one side of the crowd. He wasn't surprised to see Cal and Micco in full uniform.

"Hi, guys," Andy said, rubbing his hands in the cool morning air. "Who arranged for the military honors burial?" he asked.

"I did," was all Cal said. His friend deserved a military funeral honors detail.

Drums began as four soldiers in service dress uniform carried Luther's coffin to where his family sat waiting. The colors of the United States burial flag draped over the coffin were bright in the morning sun.

Cal looked over and saw Mary sitting next to Jamie and the kids. Luther's son, Riley, stood up a little ways away from his mother, but Jamie held Josie close to her. Mary seemed composed, but dabbed at her eyes with a handkerchief.

The coffin was gently placed on the stand. Then, the minister stood at the head and began to speak.

"Ashes to ashes, dust to dust..." the older man droned on toward the end. Cal knew Luther wasn't very religious, but Jamie insisted the kids were brought up in Sunday School at a church in Bend.

The Guard fired their rifles as *Taps* was played and the funeral flag was systematically folded. One soldier presented the flag to Jamie.

Then, the minister announced, "The family has planned a gathering at the Methodist Church's reception hall."

Andy leaned over to Cal and said, "I've got an appointment at Holt Construction after this. Want to come along?"

"Absolutely. Just give me a minute."

Cal walked a little closer to Luther's family.

Fire Chief Lockhart went up to Riley and handed him Luther's helmet and badge. "Your dad was one of our bravest firefighters, son. He will be missed."

Riley took the items and held them close to his chest,

tears streaming down his young face. Others came up to Jamie to offer their condolences and then left.

Leaning down, Cal said softly, "Will you be okay?"

Mary looked over at him. "I'll stay with her. I'm surprised Luther's parents are not here."

"I'm not," Jamie said before reaching down to wipe Josie's eyes. "Come on kids, we need to get home."

As Cal was about to leave, he looked up at a rise in the distance and saw a man wearing a trench coat, hat and sunglasses. He was amazed the man hadn't joined the crowd, if he knew Luther. But then, maybe he was just visiting another grave and decided to watch.

CHAPTER 36

THE HOLT CONSTRUCTION BUILDING was a huge three-story brick and mortar structure, with a warehouse on one end. In the yard sat numerous heavy pieces of equipment, like road graders and bulldozers, waiting for construction projects.

When Call arrived, Andy was already there, leaning against his police cruiser in uniform with his arms and legs crossed. He was parked next to a Mercedes sedan with the Holt logo on the side.

He got out of his Jeep and joined his friend.

Andy said, "Are you thinking what I'm thinking?"

Cal nodded. "This isn't over yet." He was glad his friend also believed that Bobby Crystal may be innocent.

As they walked to the entrance, Andy took off his sunglasses and said, "I found out a bit more about Jerry Holt. He owned the plastics building that went up in flames - the one where Luther was injured."

Cal looked up at the building. "That explains how Holt

got the money to build this monstrosity." Then, he added, "Let's hope he hasn't heard about Bobby's arrest."

When the two men entered the front door, Andy said softly, "Remember, you're only here as my backup."

"Eyes and ears, my friend," Cal said with a smile.

A young blonde receptionist was talking into her headphones to someone on the phone. "I'll be sure to let Mr. Holt know you called, Mr. Gillespie. I'm sorry for the delay on that job."

She looked up at Cal and Andy. "May I help you?"

"We'd like to see Jerry Holt," Andy said, showing his badge.

"Do you have an appointment?"

"Yes. We're here about Luther Greeves."

The woman's eyes teared up a bit, which she quickly wiped away and looked up at the two men. "Luther was such a great guy...I'll miss him."

"Did anyone here have issues with Luther?" Cal asked. He ignored Andy's glare.

"Not really, he got along with everyone."

"How long did Luther work here?" Andy added.

"Just eight months."

She pushed an intercom button to announce them to Holt's secretary, and then directed them to the office on the top floor.

When Cal and Andy entered the elevator., Cal shrugged and said, "Secretaries know more of what's going on in any business..."

THE STERILE-LOOKING OFFICE was bare of any paintings or personal items. The large man sitting behind the glass desk didn't rise, but greeted them with a big smile. He reminded Cal of a car salesman he knew.

"I'm Jerry Holt. What can I do for you?" the man asked in a business tone.

"I'm Andy Shaw with the County Sheriff's office. This is Cal Jamison. We have a few questions about Luther Greeves."

"I read about his death," Holt said cautiously, looking at Andy's credentials. He leaned back in his black leather chair.

Cal said, "We're trying to find out what happened to him."

"Please, have a seat."

"How well did you know Luther before he came to work for you?" Andy asked as he and Cal sat in stiff plastic chairs across from the man with graying hair.

Holt said, "I hardly spoke to him. He kept to himself, arrived each day on time and did his job."

Cal said, "This is a nice building, Mr. Holt. You've done well for yourself."

The older man smiled. "Yes, I have."

Andy then interjected, "We understand that you owned Hawk Plastics."

Holt hesitated, then said, "Yes…"

"The fire investigator's report noted that the sprinkler system in that building did not engage during the fire a year ago," Andy said.

"I had explained that it was being repaired at the time. What does that have to do with Luther?"

Cal looked at Andy. This was news to him. He couldn't hold back any longer. "Isn't it strange that Luther was almost killed in that fire and then he was murdered in another."

Holt shot up. "Murdered?"

Andy stood up. "Calm yourself, Mr. Holt. We're not saying that you did it. We just need to talk with some of his co-workers. Would that be possible now?"

The man sat back in his chair, looking a little relieved. "Yes. I'll have my foreman meet you in the warehouse."

After they left Holt's office, Andy said, "I thought we agreed you were here as my backup."

Cal shrugged and smiled. "I'm sorry…I just want to get the bastard who killed Luther."

Andy nodded. "So do I, but we have to be careful."

In the hallway, Marvin Gould, Holt's warehouse foreman, greeted them. He was a burly man with sandy hair and tattoos on his beefy arms. "I hear you want to talk to my men," he said in a raspy voice. He handed both men a blue hard hat. "You'll need to wear these where we're going."

Andy nodded and introduced himself and Cal.

THE FOREMAN LED THEM to the large warehouse. While Andy talked with Gould, Cal walked around the facility. Along the wide aisles were large wooden pallets of steel rebar and shelves filled with various sized shrink-wrapped boxes that went up to the tall ceiling. He had to move out of the way of a driver on a forklift carrying pallets of cement bags to a waiting truck at the loading dock.

Cal questioned a couple of Luther's co-workers, but they didn't really have much to say. One thought Luther was a hard man to get to know – kept pretty much to himself. Cal continued down one of the aisles where large steel drums were stacked high on pallets.

"What're you doing here?" a man's voice said behind him.

When Cal turned, he saw a tall, muscular, fair-skinned man with black hair and beard and light blue eyes.

"I'm here with the police," Cal said, unwilling to give out his own name. "We're just checking with people who worked with Luther Greeves - to see if anyone knows what happened to him."

The man then smiled and extended a hand. "I'm Ray Walker. Luther and I were good buddies."

"How well did you know him?"

"We'd have lunch a few times, when he didn't go home to his family. I've been here about the same time as Luther."

"Can you tell me if there was anyone here who had a reason to want Luther dead?"

"Nope," Walker said as a truck loaded with pallets of gypsum drywall pulled up and honked. "I have to get this."

Cal watched as Walker went up to the driver and signed for the delivery. Then, the man turned back to Cal and added, "Luther was a great guy – sometimes I hunted with him."

Cal frowned, but didn't say anything.

Just then, Andy called out, "We have to go."

OUTSIDE, THE TWO MEN compared notes.

"I didn't get much," Cal said, looking back at Ray Walker, who was now walking back into the warehouse. "How about you?"

Andy shook his head. "No. Seemed like everyone liked Luther."

"Well, he was a great guy," Cal said, quoting the young receptionist.

"Wait a minute," Andy said. He went to his vehicle, got his camera from the back seat and took photos of a license plate and tires on a dark Land Rover parked in the employees parking lot.

CHAPTER 37

FRUSTRATED AT THE DEAD ends Luther's murder seemed to be turning up, Cal decided to drive back to the crime scene and have another look around.

As he approached the area where the campsite stood, he was surprised to see the familiar motorcycle with the sidecar parked nearby. He looked around, but didn't see anyone. The blood stains on the ground he'd seen before were now mostly washed away by the rain.

"Under three minutes, just as I thought," he heard a woman's voice call out.

He turned and saw the medical examiner running towards him in a purple jogging suit, checking her watch.

"Dr. Hansen. What're you doing here?" Cal asked.

She stopped and looked up, startled at first to see him. Placing her hands on her hips, she said, "Jordan, please. I guess I could ask you the same thing."

"I'm still troubled about this case. It wasn't a typical homicide."

"Me, too." He was surprised she wasn't out of breath.

"What were you timing?" he asked.

"How long it might take to run half a mile out here in this terrain."

He thought for a moment. "You were checking to see if a man could fire a shot, then get to the target in a short amount of time."

"Yes."

"You said half a mile. That's over eight hundred yards. Which way did you run?"

"To the west."

Cal nodded. "A sniper might've stationed himself there, depending on the time of day."

"But, based on Luther's time of death, it was probably still dark."

He thought about this as they began to walk in the opposite direction she'd been running. "Did you bring your dog?"

She nodded and said, "Tut is out seeking."

"For another cadaver?"

Smiling, she said, "He's also a Search and Rescue dog for the County."

"I bet the deputies didn't search out this far from the campsite," Cal said, looking out over the landscape.

After a while, Cal knew he had to ask. "I was in the sheriff's office when your post-mortem report came in. Was Luther really alive when he was put on that pyre?"

"Yes," she said softly. "At the end of my autopsy, before we had the CO test results, I found traces of soot in his trachea. That wasn't definitive proof, but it was a pretty good indicator that at least a breath or two of smoke was taken at some point. The test confirmed it."

They walked in silence. The vegetation was more dense now. The sagebrush was thicker and larger around their legs and Juniper and Pine trees stood on a horizon.

"If that cougar was killed in the dark," Cal said at last, "the shooter must've had a thermal scope."

East of where they were walking, a dog barked consistently with a high-pitched tone.

"Come on," Jordan yelled and began to run. "That's Tut's signal for when he's found something."

THE BELGIAN SHEPHERD STOOD at a small clearing in the trees at the top of a ridge. They stopped just outside of the area so they didn't disturb any evidence.

"Tut, come," she called softly to the dog. "Good boy," she cooed as he came over and sat next to her. She reached down and scratched his head.

Cal carefully stepped as he looked around. He noticed a few footprints near some shrubs. He stopped when he saw the bi-pod marks of a sniper's rifle.

Watching Cal, she asked, "What is it?"

"Probably the sniper's hide." He quickly took some shots of the imprints with his phone camera.

Jordan looked behind them and said, "This is about the same distance from the campsite that I ran earlier."

He made a loop around the perimeter. When something caught his eye to the right, Cal slowly inched forward. "Do you have an evidence bag?" he asked as he lifted a branch of sagebrush and took more photos.

"Absolutely," Jordan said.

She ordered Tut to stay. then walked towards Cal. From her jacket pocket, she excitedly took out a pair of gloves, some tweezers and a plastic bag.

"This doesn't make sense," Cal said. "No self-respecting sniper I know would be stupid enough to leave something like this behind."

"He probably started running to the campsite as soon

as he took the shot," she said as she knelt down and bagged the cartridge case. "And, it was dark."

When she showed it to Cal, he said, "That's a .338 Lapua Magnum – the same type of bullet found in the cougar." Looking around, he said, "The rifle was a bolt-action to eject the cartridge this distance."

Jordan stood up. "Maybe the killer didn't care if he got caught."

They continued searching for a while longer, then started to return to the campsite. Tut led the way.

Jordan said, "I identified the weapon used to torture Luther as something like a Fairbairn-Sykes fighting knife."

"Those were used in WWII," Cal said.

"Yes, I checked the history of those knives."

She held up the evidence bag. "After I stop at home and change, I'll take this to the State Police Crime Lab. I just hope forensics can get some fingerprints."

"They'll be able to compare the casing to Bobby's rifle."

As they walked back to their vehicles, Jordan's phone buzzed.

When she only smiled, Cal remembered their time alone in the morgue. He appreciated anyone who found pleasure in the simplest things in life.

After the phone stopped vibrating, she said, "My house is on the way to the crime lab, and I have to change before I take these in." She put on her helmet and asked, "Would you like to see where I live?"

"Okay," Cal said, surprising himself.

CHAPTER 38

TAILING THE BLACK MOTORCYCLE, Cal shook his head. He knew he was curious about this woman, but not sure why. Maybe it was the red hair, but there was something about her that didn't quite fit into one of the boxes in his mind. His job in the Marines taught him to read people quickly, but this woman baffled him.

As they turned onto Powell Butte Road, a two-story building came into view sitting among old growth Ponderosa Pine trees. The house had a bank of large bay windows along one side. A small, detached cottage sat behind the house. Off to the right, Cal was surprised to see a large airplane hangar near a grass airstrip.

They parked their vehicles in front of the garage. As he got out of his Jeep, Cal saw a 1958 red Corvette roadster convertible with the white bullets on each side parked in one of the bays.

"That's my favorite summer car," she said as she took off her helmet. Tut jumped out of the sidecar and ran toward a water bowl near the house's back door.

"How long have you had your bike?" he asked.

"Four years. I found it listed in the Trash and Treasures section of the Antique Motorcycle Club magazine."

"When I went to Klamath Falls to meet Luther's parents, I ran into a group called the Oregon Trail Chapter of that club."

She smiled and said, "I'm a member."

Cal nodded toward the hangar and asked, "Who's the pilot?"

She smiled and said, "I am."

Tut ran back to Jordan and barked.

"Come on in," she said as she walked toward the house. "Tut's hungry."

THEY ENTERED A MUD room. Following her lead, he took off his shoes and coat, then walked into the kitchen. The bright room was open with a large island in the center. Tall white cabinets reached up toward the high ceiling.

"Welcome to my humble home," Jordan said as she filled Tut's bowl with dry food. The dog quickly ate every nugget.

"He has a healthy appetite," Cal said.

"Always, since he was a pup." She took two mugs from a glass-fronted cupboard and said, "I have a Keurig, so help yourself to some coffee or tea while I change."

Jordan ran up the stairs to the left of the kitchen and Tut left the room.

Cal admired that everything was neat and in its place. He smiled when he saw that she used San Francisco Bay pods. He never really liked the idea of the Keurig coffee makers because of the landfill waste, but these pods had a mesh pouch around the grounds, instead of the usual plastic. As the dark coffee brewed, he thankfully inhaled the strong aroma.

Sipping the strong Espresso blend, he walked into the spacious living room. Sunlight streamed in through tall, south-facing windows. Big leather furniture and rustic barnwood tables dotted the room, creating various seating areas. To the right was a large couch, and Tut lay on a big pillow next to the wide river-rock fireplace. Interestingly, there was no television in the room.

Looking around, he didn't see any evidence of others living there. In the mud room, he'd noticed there hadn't been any men's shoes or jackets. On the mantle, there was only one photo of an older couple. He assumed they were probably Jordan's parents.

Cal went to a tall bookcase and looked at a few of the book spines. Agatha Christie seemed to be a favorite author, as well as J.A. Jance. In the non-fiction section were various books on medicine, forensics, and, interestingly, both plane and auto mechanics.

He heard footsteps and turned. Jordan now wore jeans and a red sweater. Her hair was wet and pulled up into a ponytail. She went to the kitchen and brewed herself a cup of coffee, then came over to join him. A whiff of lavender followed her.

"I love mysteries," she said. "Don't you?"

"Sometimes, I've felt that my life has been a series of them, sort of like the character in a Clive Cussler novel."

She looked up at him and asked, "What does that mean?"

He shrugged, took another swig and stepped away toward a window. He saw the hangar and asked, "What plane do you have?"

"I have two - a '48 Stinson and a red and silver Carbon Cub, which needs some work. The Cub is a fun bush plane that I will be able to pretty much land anywhere. I've had the Stinson since I graduated med school. I like to take it to various antique air shows, like the one in McMinnville - where the Spruce Goose is now located."

Cal turned and said, "I have a Skyhawk 172 that I maintain myself, but I've never totally restored a plane before." He was surprised he was actually jealous of this woman.

"Well, isn't that a funny coincidence," she said. "We're both pilots."

They stood for some time talking about flying and sipping their coffee. Cal felt as if they'd been friends for years.

Then, out of the blue, he said, "I also like to fly fish, when I'm not investigating a friend's murder."

"I've never done that," she said.

"Maybe I could show you how sometime."

"Where do you live?" she asked.

"I'm currently with my grandparents in Tumalo while on medical leave," was all he said.

Then, Jordan looked at a clock on the mantel. "It's time to go."

She laid some kindling and logs in the fireplace. "I'll light these when I get back," she said and walked to the kitchen.

Cal followed her and set his mug in the sink.

Jordan put on her leather jacket and wrapped a white silk scarf around her neck. Then, she turned and grinned at him. "Well, I'd better get the evidence to the lab."

OUTSIDE, AS THEY PASSED the hangar, Cal asked, "What's wrong with the Cub?"

Excitedly, Jordan said, "When I bought it, the right rear wing spar was bent from a ground loop. The gear and

158

struts appeared to be undamaged, but I got it for a significant discount. Now, I just have to tear down the wing, replace the spar, then recover the wing and put it back on the plane. It'll be good as new."

"You're going to do this yourself?"

She smiled as she answered, "Of course!"

Cal smiled and nodded.

"Thanks for your help today," he said. "It means a lot to me. I finally feel like we're getting somewhere on Luther's case."

She placed her hand on his arm and said, "We'll find out who did this to your friend."

"See you around," Cal said, got into his Jeep and drove away.

CHAPTER 39

THE NEXT DAY, MARY drove Winnie to the Crooked River area to gather materials for her oil paintings. As she drove, Winnie regaled her with some history of the area.

"The Jamison Ranch was founded by Glenn's ancestor back in the early 1800s who came west after immigrating from Scotland. Glenn loves to tell the stories of how Callum Jamison had helped to build the Oregon Trail. We will get to the river through the Jamison land."

Winnie pointed to the east at the jutting volcanic formation in the distance.

"There are two versions of how Smith Rock got its name – one is of a man called Smith who fell from the ledge and died. Another story said it was named after an Indian Agent named John Smith. My parents called it the 'Animal Village' because of all the plants and animals there. It is made up of Clarno ash, basalt, and tuff formations millions of years old and was left standing when a large caldera collapsed around it. The Crooked River runs through it. We will go to Smith Rock another day."

"It's beautiful! What is the elevation at the top?" Mary asked.

"Over three thousand feet." Winnie laughed. "When I was a child, my brother and I loved to run along the River Trail for a great view of the rock called 'Monkey Face.' We would have picnics up there with my parents after we gathered our herbs and roots. Good memories..."

After Winnie told Mary to turn left onto another road, she asked, "Where do you live?"

"Seattle," Mary said. "I love the city, but the population is growing and there is so much traffic now."

"And, it rains a lot there," Winnie said with a chuckle. "You won't get a lot of rain or traffic in Central Oregon."

"It is gorgeous here."

"How did you get interested in art?"

"I have to say it was my father – he loved historic buildings, and I would go with him when he had discovered some old beauty that needed restoration. I began drawing while he worked."

"Do you think you will stay in Seattle?"

Mary thought for a moment, then said, "I'm not sure..."

AS THEY PASSED UNDER the tall sign for the Jamison Ranch, they went over the cattle guard and up the long dirt lane toward an enormous log home. An older man came out of a barn to meet them. He opened Winnie's door and said, "Well, I never thought I'd see you here, Wyanet."

Winnie took his hand and got out of the car. She hugged the man and said, "We came to gather some materials for our paintings."

She turned and introduced him to Mary, using his Paiute name. "This is Wesa, Micco's dad and my cousin."

Mary went up to him and shook his hand. "I'm Mary. I met your son recently at the D&D."

"That's his favorite breakfast place."

When he saw Winnie looking around nervously, Wes said, "She went into town."

Winnie sighed in relief, then she saw the confusion on Mary's face. "I'll explain to you later."

She turned to her cousin and said, "We want to drive down to the river."

"Take the old wagon road – you know the way."

THE WOMEN GOT BACK into the car and drove east along another dirt road. Eventually, the road became more of a small path with two narrow ruts dug into the soil.

"How did you and Glenn meet?" Mary asked as she swerved to miss hitting a rock, thankful that she'd gotten the insurance for her rental car.

"It was at a summer festival in Bend. Did you know it was originally called 'Farewell Bend' by the early settlers? Vendors line the streets with goods and there's food and music and dancing. I was working at one of the food tents with a cousin when this burly, red-headed young man who looked like a logger came up and introduced himself. We've been together ever since."

Winnie grew quiet as she gazed out over the land. The blue sky and striking cumulus clouds formed a canopy over the brown grassland, which was dotted with golden rabbitbrush and Western juniper. The dark hills in the distance were shadowed from the sun by the clouds.

"Is this really a wagon trail?" Mary asked to break the silence.

"Yes. Each time I go along here, I think of the people who risked their lives to come west in search of a better life. Some never made it. Some of them were nice, but many were evil - especially to my people." She shivered and placed her arms around herself. "But the Jamison family were different, we mattered to them. We have always been like any other person to them. They respect us – they respect the land."

Mary was silent for a long while, not sure what to say. "I'm so sorry. I can't imagine what life was like then," was all she could think of as she followed Winnie's gaze.

"I was born on the Warm Springs Reservation, so I never had to live what some did. But, my grandfather told me stories of that time - of how we once had been free..."

Mary glanced at the older woman sitting next to her, her weathered face tanned and lined. Her deep brown eyes looked ahead, seeing much farther than the nearby hills.

Winnie sighed, slapped her hands on the blue cotton dress that covered her knees and said, "Yet, I believe the lessons of the past help us to shape the future we now live."

They continued in silence until the wagon trail faded and they turned onto a road that went down to the Crooked River's edge. Mary parked the car and opened the trunk. They took out a couple of buckets with bags and tools Winnie had brought along.

While the two women walked along the riverbank, the older woman talked more about her home growing up on the reservation to the west of the canyon.

"The property stretches from the Cascades Mountains to the tall cliffs along the Deschutes River in Crook County. Some of the Paiutes have been there since 1869."

As they walked, Winnie shared stories from her past. "As a child, I watched when our people ground plants and small pieces of rocks they had gathered into different colors of powder. They would then mix paints with it, which they used on their bodies for ceremonies. That is how I learned to create natural pigments in my art."

They took samples of some of the rocks, soils and plants as Winnie explained about each one. She picked up a rock. "This is a jasper," she said as she rubbed the rough edge against a larger rock to reveal the red color. Turning the stone over in her hand, she pointed to some veins of yellow. "It can also have a yellow tint, depending on the minerals in it."

"This is so fascinating. Exactly what I was looking for."

"Red is the color of life," Winnie said as she handed it to Mary, who ran her finger over the stone, then placed it in her small canvas bag that was slung across her body.

Winnie continued surveying the land as she explained the process. "First you must wash the sample and let it fully dry in the sun. Then place the rock between a sheet of canvas or heavy plastic to pound it into smaller pieces in order to grind it into a powder. Sift and wash again several times before storing the pigment. I have found that I like to use those paper coffee filters for the last drying process – it is easier to scrape off the fine pigment."

"This is similar to the paints used for frescos I studied in Europe," Mary said excitedly.

"Exactly!" Winnie smiled. "But I have only seen those paintings in pictures in library books." After a bit, she added, "Rocks are a lot like history books. Depending on where they are found, they tell stories of the earth's past."

As they walked on, Mary loved the feeling of the warm sun on her skin. Memories flooded her of when she was young, growing up on her parents' small ranch near Bend with her sister, Jamie. It was a time when her little family had been happy. *Yes*, she thought, *I could get used to this again.*

When they came to the lower riverbed, Winnie squatted, removed a rock hammer and chisel from one bucket and began to chip at some dark-colored material.

Mary watched as Winnie picked up one loose piece and handed it to her. "What is this?" she asked.

"Petrified wood. It is a good color, no?"

"It's beautiful."

Winnie gently wrapped the fossil in newspaper, then gave it to the younger woman to put in her bag.

Eagerly, Mary continued to search the area. Something caught her eye and she knelt down to slowly inch a rock from its resting place.

"Ah," Winnie said, looking over Mary's shoulder. "You found a Red Plume Agate. Very nice."

"What a fun treasure hunt!" Mary exclaimed.

WHEN THEY RETURNED TO the Jamison Ranch, Mary saw two men and Wes talking near the barn.

"I need to stop and say goodbye to Wes," Winnie said.

As Mary parked the car near the log house, a striking tall, robust woman with gray streaks in her long brunette hair walked towards them from the garage next to the log home. She was in jeans and a blue Western-style shirt, worn boots, tan leather gloves, and a black hat.

"Oh, no," Winnie sighed.

"What?" Mary asked.

"I was hoping we could get away before she got back," the older woman said softly to Mary before they got out of the car. Winnie didn't like the family feud between the Jamisons, but she had to honor Glenn's wishes about his family.

"Hello, Winnie," the woman said. "It's so good to see you." She turned to Mary, took off a leather glove and reached out her hand. "I'm Nina Jamison."

Mary shook the stunning woman's hand. "I'm Mary Creswell. Winnie has been so kind in teaching me about the colored minerals in this area. I'm an artist, visiting my sister."

"Can you stay for a bit?" Nina asked as she began to walk towards the house. "I have some lemonade in the house."

Winnie quickly said, "I'm sorry, but we have to go."

Nina turned and said, "Oh…How is Glenn? I would like to come see him sometime—"

"He is well, thank you."

Just then, Mary saw the big man with a chiseled face, red hair and beard walking from the barn with the man in a suit. She overheard the suited man say, "Well, Jack, I can see this land becoming a great destination for tourists who want to see what's it like to spend time on a working ranch."

Winnie quickly turned to Mary. "Let's go, dearie."

THE TWO WOMEN GOT into Mary's car and left.

When they turned onto Route 97, Winnie said, "I must apologize, but, Glenn doesn't like me spending much time at the ranch."

Mary had been surprised at the abrupt departure, but felt it wasn't her place to pry. She had hoped to get to know Cal's mother better.

"Who were those men back there?" she asked.

Winnie said, "The younger man is Cal's brother, Jack. I don't know who the other was."

As she drove, Mary's thoughts shifted to the big man with the red hair. He seemed very different from Cal.

CHAPTER 40

CAL WAS IN THE makeshift gym he'd set up in one bay of Glenn's garage when he started therapy. He wanted to get his full strength back and was frustrated when his shoulder still wouldn't let him do his usual twenty pull-ups without some resistance. Despite the pain, he continued to push through. He'd been at this for about an hour now and was sweating profusely.

"You're not as young as you were in boot camp, soldier," he said to his reflection in a mirror covering one wall. He could still hear his drill sergeant's voice in his head.

As he finished his exercise circuit with some pushups, he thought about his time in San Diego. Marine Recruit Training was a grueling thirteen-week program that he'd excelled at. His life working on the big ranch and playing sports in high school helped to prepare him for most of what he'd be up against. He always liked a challenge and the Crucible Event at the end was his favorite. With little sleep and food supplies, he and his team had to undergo assigned tasks, eventually relying on each other to make sure they all succeeded.

When Cal did his last pushup, he wiped down the gym equipment. Then he washed his face in the small sink and changed into a clean T-shirt before going up to Micco's room.

HOW WAS THE WORKOUT?" Micco asked Cal from his desk.

"A little better today. I wish we had a pool here. Back in high school, I was on both the football and swim team, but water polo was my favorite."

"That's why you were so good at boot camp," Micco laughed. "The first time I saw you swim in the ocean, you were crazy fast! I always wondered if you weren't part fish."

"Ah, those were the days."

Cal went to the sink and drank a large glass of water. Then, he went over to look at the white board - what he now liked to think of as the 'evidence board.'

Micco was smiling as he started typing on his computer keyboard.

"So, to recap," Cal said, "what we have so far, are my photos of the crime scene I took before the sheriff arrived."

"Which was illegal," Micco cut in.

Cal turned and added, "Your background info on Luther, which was probably also illegal, and Amanda's photos. I'm glad she sent me another copy, since I gave the first set to the sheriff."

Cal handed Micco his phone and said, "There are some photos on this I took yesterday." He filled his friend in on the evidence he and Jordan had found at the crime scene.

"Don't forget your notes on Bobby Crystal's arrest,"

Micco added as he downloaded the new images onto his computer.

"Damn it! I feel like something's missing…something about Bobby that's bothering me."

Micco only nodded as he printed the images.

"Glenn and I are going to the fire station later," Cal said. "I want to see if anyone has a different version of what happened at last year's fire."

"You might want to take a shower first."

Cal sniffed one armpit and laughed. "I might."

"I've been doing some digging into Luther's military record." Micco turned the monitor and said, "Check this out."

Cal looked at the computer screen. "Interesting. I didn't know he was a 'FISTer' in the Army."

"Yep, that's what Forward Observers are called. Basically, they direct the heavier artillery fire to an enemy's target. They work independently behind enemy lines for weeks at a time. Luther was commander of a three-man team."

Micco clicked on a link and brought up a new screen. "This is from one of his teams' attacks – east of Baghdad of a known terrorist cell." He printed the screen, then added, "The mission was a success."

Cal read the new information. "I was in that area…"

Micco pointed to a paragraph he'd highlighted on the screen. "Interestingly, all of Luther's team are now dead, except one."

"Do you know who that is?"

"Not yet. I'm still checking."

"How?" Cal asked. "You don't have military clearance anymore."

Micco smiled and winked. "I know a guy."

CHAPTER 41

GLENN WAS WAITING BY his old Buick as Cal drove up to the Bend Fire Station. The car was a '58 green and white classic Roadmaster that Glenn had bought new.

"You could've ridden with me," Cal said as he got out of his vehicle.

Glenn patted the hood of his Buick. "This baby rides better than your little Jeep."

It was quiet when they walked inside the tall red-brick building.

"Gordon's office is back here," Glenn said.

The fire chief sat behind his desk going over some paperwork. Cal knew he'd been the captain of the Los Angeles Arson Squad before moving to Bend. Gordon Lockhart was a stocky man with red hair. He looked up when the two men entered.

"Well, I'll be damned," Lockhart said as he rose to his feet. "What're you doing here, old man?"

Glenn chuckled. "Talk fer yourself! I thought you said you were retiring at our poker game last Friday."

"I always say that to get you off my back. Norma and me are building that house near Redmond. When it's finished, I'm leaving."

Lockhart looked at Cal. "Hello, son. How're you doing?"

"Good, thank you, sir." Cal looked around. "Is Karen Burke here today?"

"Yep, she's out back washing down the Medic Unit vehicle we just had out on a call."

Cal nodded and turned toward the door. As he left, he heard Lockhart say, "Good to see you're still alive, old man…"

OUTSIDE, CAL STOPPED DEAD when he saw the muscular young woman with short brown hair. He felt as if he'd been kicked in the gut. The woman reminded him of Sarah Leisner – the only woman he'd ever let into his heart. She was an Army Medic that he'd met in 2007 when he was injured by an IED during an assignment between Fallujah and Ramadi, Iraq.

Sarah was a sweet girl from Virginia, with a brother who was also in the military. Cal received some shrapnel in one leg in that blast that she removed and bandaged. They'd spent a few months getting to know each other. Then, just as she was about to go home, their camp was bombed and he'd lost her.

Cal tried to shake off the memory as he walked over to Karen. He was surprised she was alone, hosing off the vehicle. They'd only met a couple of times at the D&D when he was having lunch with Luther. The young woman smiled as he came near.

"Hi, Karen." Looking around, he asked, "Can I give you a hand?"

"No, sir, I have it." She turned off the hose and turned to him with her hands on her hips. "What can I do for you?"

"Please, call me Cal." He stood with his hands in his pockets to put her at ease. "You have a great smile."

"Thank you."

She still seemed on guard, so he got to the point. "I understand you were in the military before training as a firefighter."

"Yes, sir...er, Cal." She smiled again. "Sorry...habit. I was in the Army for eight years - a Medic in Kuwait for three." Her face changed and she looked away for a few seconds. He knew that look - he saw it in the mirror most days.

"I couldn't wait to get out of that shithole," she finally said. "But, the training for this job was much harder than anything I ever did over there."

"What do you mean?"

"As a Medic, I had to go through basic training, plus sixteen weeks AIT at Fort Sam Houston in Texas. Once I got my Combat Medic Specialist rating, I was sent overseas. This job requires much more physical ability, which is now my new lifestyle. I have to keep my strength up to do everything a firefighter's job requires - with full gear on. It's not just bodybuilding, it's aerobic stamina and endurance, as well." She smiled and added, "I love this job!"

"And, we appreciate you doing this..." He cleared his throat and said, "I'm trying to find out who killed Luther Greeves."

She only nodded.

Cal continued, "I know about him losing his memory from that fire last year."

"Yes, after that mezzanine fell on him and Jeremy...Luther was in so much pain during his therapy.

He never was the same man after that."

"You were at that fire with him?"

Karen nodded and quickly glanced at the station. Cal figured she was thinking about the loss of the fire chief's son. "I should've been the one to go in with Luther."

"Can you tell me anything about that fire?"

Karen leaned in and said softly, "It was no accident…"

He looked around to make sure they weren't overheard. "Why do you say that?"

"The fire investigator determined it was probably started by faulty wiring in the office area, but he said it was really hard to tell. When I was able to go in, there was something odd about that mezzanine. To me, it went down too quickly."

"Why didn't you say anything?"

"I told Luther."

CHAPTER 42

BETTY NOLAN WAS EXCITED when she returned to the newspaper building after a lunch interview with a local author. She loved being a journalist, but for now, she put her notes aside and turned on her computer. She had some investigative research to do first.

She began searching through old records, using both Luther Greeves and Jeremy Lockhart's names. She noted the dates on the fires they'd worked on and was surprised to see that Jeremy had only joined the Deschutes County Fire Department a year before his death.

Betty stumbled onto a story she'd written when Karen Burke had joined the fire department. She had been impressed with Karen being the first woman on the force, especially after her military experience as a Medic overseas. Betty quickly made a note of the dates that both Jeremy and Karen were assigned to Luther's team.

Sighing because she had digressed a bit, Betty started looking at dates of other fires in which Luther was mentioned. Luther's team was always the first responders on most fires in the area.

There was one story about Luther going into the Army in 2000. Then, she searched through records that went back to 1997, when she found her article on Luther and Jamie Creswell's marriage. She smiled when she saw their wedding photo, they looked so happy.

Before '97, there were a few arrests mentioned for disorderly conduct, but they'd been dismissed. Betty made a note to contact her friend at the Klamath Falls police station about those.

She got up and stretched, realizing that she'd been sitting at the computer for over two hours. She smiled as she walked to the break room to get a strong cup of tea. This was how she worked when she became engrossed in a story. She'd lose all track of time as she delved into other peoples' lives.

When she retired from teaching and became a reporter in 1995, she built a good relationship with the local police and often learned things before they became public. She'd go to the police station every day and copy down the latest arrests. She earned their respect by reporting accurately on the officials' efforts to prevent and solve crimes.

Betty smiled as she walked back toward her desk.

"What's got you so happy?" a voice said behind her.

Startled, Betty almost spilled her tea. "Josh! I thought I was alone back here."

Josh Barr was another reporter for the Bend Gazette. He laughed and said, "You're never alone in a room full of newspaper reporters. Did you finish your article on Robert Crystal's arrest for today's press release?"

"Absolutely. My interview with Sheriff Morrow was interesting and the officials feel they have their man."

"Well," Josh said, turning off his computer, "I'm done

for the day. See you tomorrow."

Betty looked at the clock and went back to her research. She never knew if a tidbit of info would be important, so she included everything in her searches... She always made notes on any scrap piece of paper she could find, including napkins, knowing she'd organize them all later and write a discernible composite of the events.

She rotated her aching shoulders, took off her glasses and leaned back in her chair. It was getting late and she had an early interview the next morning with the local animal rescue shelter, but she knew that she was close to finding something important on Luther. Sighing, she put her glasses back on and started looking for articles written the previous year.

Suddenly, she stopped when she saw a headline: *Unexplained Wildfire on BLM Land*, with a photo above the article. The rough terrain was in flames, smoke billowing skyward as the firefighters were trying to contain it. It had been reported by some hunters near China Hat.

"That's interesting!" Betty said out loud and called Cal.

CAL ARRIVED SHORTLY AT the newspaper office. The receptionist knew he was coming, so he went to the back where Betty's desk was located. He was glad they were alone in the large newsroom.

"That was quick," Betty said.

"I was nearby when you called." He didn't mention that he'd been sitting in his vehicle outside of the fire station, looking at a photo on his phone of the one woman he'd ever loved.

He sat in a chair next to Betty's desk. "What've you got for me?"

She leaned in and said softly, "I thought that, with Bobby's arrest, Luther's case was closed. But, you seem to think otherwise."

He looked around and answered, "Yep, but please keep it under your hat for now."

Betty showed Cal the printed story. "Well, I found this fire was started southwest of Brothers. And, if I'm not mistaken, it was not too far from where Luther's body was found."

He looked at the photo. The starting point of the wildfire was eerily constructed like the pyre he'd seen when he found Luther. As he read, he saw that the cause was later determined as a road flare. Then, he looked at the date on the article.

"You may be on to something," he said. "Can I take this with me?"

"Sure thing. It's a copy."

"You're a peach, Betty." He folded the paper and placed it in his jacket pocket. "Thanks."

"No. Thank you for giving me a chance to help. And, possibly a scoop on Luther Greeves?"

Cal smiled. "We'll see." Then his phone rang and bagpipes began playing *Scotland the Brave*. "Damn it!" he said. "Micco changed my ringtone again. That's why he was smiling this morning."

"You could let it play a bit," Betty said, dancing in her chair. "I love Scottish music."

Sighing, he answered it.

"This is Mary," the voice at the other end said. "I'm still at the gallery and wondered if you're available to meet me somewhere for dinner…is tonight too soon?"

Cal thought for a moment, then said, "Sure. How about the Pine Tavern…" He looked at his watch and added, "I could be there in twenty minutes."

"Perfect!" Mary said and hung up.

He saw the look of the woman sitting across the desk from him.

"Sounds like you've got a date!" Betty said.

"Just two friends…having dinner together," Cal replied. He thanked Betty again and left.

CHAPTER 43

CAL ALWAYS LIKED TO arrive early for a meeting, something he learned in his military training. He worked in Reconnaissance, so his job was to scope out the lay of the land beforehand. He never liked surprises.

When he entered the Pine Tavern, there were few people in the bar area at the front. He walked to a tall table near the window and sat down. When the blonde waitress came over, he ordered a beer.

"Also," he asked, "Would you see if a table by the back window is available? I'm meeting someone."

The waitress smiled and said, "I'll check."

While he waited, he wondered what his grandmother thought of Mary. This young woman was someone with a past that was a mystery to him.

We're just friends, he silently reminded himself. Since Sarah, Cal kept the lock on his heart shut tight.

His drink arrived and he took the news article out of his jacket pocket. Reading the report, it all seemed to him that this could have been a practice fire, to see what material was available in the area and how much would be needed to burn a specific amount of time. Luckily, it had not caused too much damage to the wildland around it, but the case had never been solved. The timing was interesting – it was a week before the fire that killed Luther.

MARY WALKED BY THE window wearing a pink summer dress, carrying a teal-colored pashmina shawl over one arm. She waved to him and came in.

"You look nice," Cal said as he stood up and helped her into one of the seats. Her skin glowed after being out in the sun.

"Thank you. I got this shawl at the Seattle airport before my flight here."

"So, how did you and Winnie get along?"

Mary sighed. "It was magical! She's a wonder and I learned so much from her."

The waitress came over and Mary ordered a glass of Brut.

"I'll have a table for you in about fifteen minutes," the young woman said.

"Thank you," Cal said, then he asked Mary, "Where did you and Winnie go?"

"Mostly along the Crooked River. I got some wonderful samples of different kinds of volcanic materials and woods. I also found what is called Limb Casts. I will add them to my rock collection…"

Mary's drink arrived and she talked excitedly, non-stop while Cal just listened.

"We stopped at Smith Rock on the way back, but didn't have time to explore the area. There was a lovely small wedding in progress when we arrived. The bride looked so beautiful in her white dress, which billowed in the warm breeze. They stood near the precipice of the deep gorge as the minister performed the small ceremony. Their only witnesses were the photographer and the minister... Winnie told me the history of Smith Rock. It was so magnificent!"

"Yes, it's one of my favorite places," Cal said.

"I have some photos—" she began, but was interrupted by the waitress, telling them their table was ready.

THE COUPLE FOLLOWED THE woman through a small hallway with little booths in alcoves on one side, then entered a large room with a giant Ponderosa Pine tree growing through it. They sat at a small table in one corner with glass windows on both sides and a small brook running below.

"Wow," Mary said after taking a sip of her drink. "This place is amazing."

"It was built in 1936 by two women," Cal said, "just after the Depression."

"I saw some of the old photos hanging on the wall as we came back here. What a great landmark."

An older waiter came up to them and handed them menus. He also placed a small bowl of hot scones on the table. He winked at Mary and said, "There's honey butter in there for you to enjoy."

"Thank you," she responded.

"My name is Steve and I'll be your server tonight."

To Mary, the waiter said, "I see you have your Korbel." He looked at Cal and asked, "Can I get anything for you to drink, sir?"

Cal said, "I'll have a Scotch and water, Steve."

"Any preference on your Scotch?"

"Glenfiddich. Thanks."

"Ah, good choice."

The waiter left and the two looked at the menu. When Steve returned with Cal's drink, they placed their order. Mary chose the seared salmon dinner and Cal ordered steak.

Alone again, Cal said, "So, Mary Creswell, tell me about yourself."

"Well, you already know I grew up here with Jamie on our parents' ranch, where Jamie lives now."

"Were your parents from this area?"

"No, Dad was an Architectural Historian. He came here from New York in the 70s, when Bend was wanting to modernize the downtown area. He and Mom met here and got married."

Steve returned with a steak knife for Cal and left.

"Then, when I was fourteen," Mary continued, "Dad got a job in Albany, New York, working to redevelop his hometown. He wanted to preserve some of the historic buildings that he grew to love as a boy, so they didn't become a parking lot."

"I think I would've liked him." When he saw the expression on her face, he added, "Jamie told me about your parents."

Mary looked out the window for a moment, then said, "I was in Paris studying art when they died."

Cal put his hand over hers. "I'm so sorry."

They sat for a moment, each dealing with their own pain of loss.

"You said you had some photos," Cal finally said, removing his hand. He took a scone from the basket and buttered it.

Mary's eyes lit up and she pulled an envelope from her purse. "I had them developed right away when I got back into town."

Putting the scone on a small plate, he wiped his hands and thumbed through the images. "These are really good."

"I like to take photos of scenery I want to paint later, so I get the colors right. I got my interest in art from my dad. When I studied in Europe – the colors there are so beautiful, but that was nothing like what I saw today."

Cal stopped on an image of a familiar setting.

"You went to The Jamison?" he asked.

"Yes, Winnie wanted me to see a few areas of the ranch on our own before we left. She said this was a special place."

He nodded, but he didn't tell her that in the background of the photo was the ridge where his dad had been killed.

When Mary saw his face, she said, "You can keep that one, if you want."

Cal slid the image into his jacket pocket while Mary buttered a scone. Then, he kept scanning the other photos.

When he saw they had also gone to a state park on the Crooked River Canyon, he said, "One of my ancestors, Callum Jamison, came to this country from Scotland with his parents. When he turned nineteen, he decided to go west to work as a fur trader and joined the Hudson's Bay Company with Peter Ogden." He showed the image to Mary and added, "This photo is of the Ogden Wayside."

"Fascinating," Mary said, then placed her chin in her hand and added, "so you were named after him?"

"Yes. It was when Callum saw this area he decided to leave the Company and create his homestead."

He looked at the image again and smiled, "Winnie looks happy here."

"I think she enjoyed that trip as much as I did." She took a small bite of scone, then said, "I even met your mother. She is so nice. But, we only stayed for a short while. Winnie seemed anxious to leave then."

Cal didn't know what to say.

"There were a couple of men there, too. I think they were talking about creating a dude ranch around there."

He took a long sip of his drink, then asked, "Was one of those men a big redhead?"

Mary smiled and said, "Yes. I think his name was Jack."

When their food arrived, Mary dove into hers. Cal only took a few bites and stopped.

"I didn't realize how hungry I am," she said. "This salmon is heaven."

She looked at Cal and asked, "Is something wrong?"

He shook his head and said, "I guess I'm not as hungry as I thought."

She smiled and continued eating.

Cal took another sip of Scotch and asked, "Where do you work in Seattle?"

Mary put her fork down and explained. "At The Henry Gallery on the University of Washington Campus. One time, I saw a painting there by Leonid Afremov, called *Paris of My Dreams*. I love the colors he used and it reminded of me of my time there."

"When do you think you'll go back?" Cal asked.

"I don't know yet."

Finished with their dinner, Cal ordered the bread pudding for dessert and two espressos.

"Now, I want to know more about you, Cal Jamison," Mary said.

He cleared his throat and drank some water. "Well, my ancestry you know. I was born on the Jamison and grew up on the Double J."

"Why both ranches?" Mary asked, placing her elbows on the table.

"When I was fifteen, I moved in with my grandparents in Tumalo." He shifted in his seat and added, "Family dynamics you don't have time for now. Then, after high school, I went into the Marines. Came back a year ago..."

He stopped there. Some things weren't meant to be discussed at dinner with a pretty woman.

CHAPTER 44

LATER, CAL WALKED MARY to her car. After saying goodnight, he realized he was glad it was over because of the awkwardness toward the end. *Why do women have to do that?* he wondered. *They like to get in your personal space.*

As he watched her drive away, he realized that he would never fully understand the female race.

On the way to his Jeep, Cal ran into Andy.

"She's pretty," his friend said, smiling. "On a date?"

"Just two people having dinner." Then, Cal quickly asked, "How's the case coming, even if it's considered closed?"

Andy looked around cautiously. "I have to be careful doing much more on it right now or the sheriff will be on my neck. We're still waiting for the ballistics report on that shell casing you and Dr. Hansen found near the crime scene. You never said what you two were doing out there…"

"We both had a hunch." When Cal saw Andy's smile,

he shook his head.

"It's about time you got back out there – dating, I mean."

"I date…sometimes."

"But they never last very long, do they?"

Anxious to change the subject, Cal said, "By the way, I was thinking – if Bobby killed Luther, he would never have left that belt buckle behind."

Andy nodded. "That makes sense."

"Micco learned something about Luther's military service. Of his three-man team in the Army, only one is still alive. I don't think that's a coincidence."

"How'd he get that information?" Andy asked.

"He has his ways…and I don't ask."

Cal was about to leave, when he remembered the article. He took it from his pocket and handed it to his friend. "Take a look at this – I'm thinking it could've been a practice fire."

Andy scanned the article and looked up. "Same area. And, it was started with a flair, too."

"Yep. Look at the date."

'Oh, you may be right."

Then, Cal added, "There's something else bothering me about one of Luther's co-workers at Holt Construction. Ray Walker. Could you look into him for me and let me know what you find out?"

"Interesting that you should ask. You saw me take photos of that Land Rover in Holt's parking lot. I looked up the license plate and it's registered to Ray Walker."

"Damn," Cal said, "I hope you plan to check the tire castings from the crime scene against that vehicle."

"I need more evidence to do that, but I'm working on it…"

CHAPTER 45

"JOIN US FOR BREAKFAST," Glenn called out from the kitchen as Cal was about to leave the next morning. He smiled and walked to where his grandparents sat every day at this time. The sun was coming in the window as it rose in the clear sky.

Cal poured a cup of coffee and sat down. He noticed that the color was coming back into Glenn's face and he was looking more like his robust self again.

"I like your Mary," Winnie said as she got up and took some bread from the toaster.

"She's not 'my' Mary," Cal corrected her. "She's Jamie's sister."

"And she certainly has an eye for art," Winnie said. She set a plate of eggs and bacon in front of Cal. "I watched her as she chose the particular soils that will enrich her oils. She reminds me of when I was first bitten by the need to paint. I think I was only eight when I drew my first picture."

Cal shook his head and laughed. "The colors Mary

wears…" he said. "I guess an artist can get away with that."

Her grandparents looked at each other.

"Are you fond of her?" Glenn asked point blank, which took Cal by surprise.

Thinking for a moment, he shrugged. "I sort of like spending time with her."

"You're not getting any younger," his grandfather teased. "Maybe it's time you settled down."

Cal thought of one woman in his past that he'd considered this with, but he immediately shut down the memory. He'd never told anyone about her. Silently, he spread some homemade apple butter on a piece of toast.

"Nina liked her," Winnie said, then she quickly glanced at Glenn, seeing how his jaw tightened. Sitting down, she was immediately sorry she'd brought up anything to do with the Jamison Ranch.

"Why would you go there?" Glenn asked.

"I had dinner with Mary last night," Cal said quickly in an attempt to sidetrack his grandfather. "We ate at the Pine Tavern."

The room was quiet for a moment, then Glenn smiled and said, "It's good you're getting out with people your age." He reached over and took one of Winnie's hands.

Relieved, Cal said to Glenn, "I wanted to ask you what Gordon talked about at the fire station."

"He told me how he met his wife, Norma, in a cooking class in San Francisco. When she saw him, she told her friend that he was the man she was going to marry."

Winnie sighed, glad to see her husband smile again.

"Norma's still working as a pastry chef at Anthony's Restaurant in the Old Mill District in Bend," the older man added.

"Did he say anything about Luther's case?" Cal asked.

"Gordon did mention how he himself was once injured

in a fire in California, when an upper level had caved in on his team. The LA authorities found their firebug had set fires all over the city. His experience was too much of a coincidence like Luther's fire, but the California one was determined to be arson."

CAL WAS UP IN Micco's room when he heard a vehicle arrive outside. Looking out the window, he saw a police cruiser and said, "Andy's here."

Micco stopped typing and said, "You'd better take down those photos you took of Luther's notes."

Quickly, Cal removed them and then opened the door. "We're up here," he called out.

"Good morning," Andy said as he climbed the stairs, carrying a folder under one arm. Once inside, he looked around the room and added, "Nice digs, Micco."

Micco shrugged and said, "It's home for now."

The detective walked to the white board and stood for a moment. "I see you two have been busy."

"What brings you here so early in the morning?" Cal asked.

"I wanted to let you know we had to let Bobby Crystal go last night," Andy said.

"What? Why?" Micco asked.

"We got the Ballistics report on the bullet from the cougar. It wasn't a match to Bobby's rifle."

Cal shook his head and smiled. "I never thought Bobby was guilty. Any news on the casing I found at the crime scene?"

"Not yet, but I've got some info for you on Ray Walker." Andy handed the folder to Cal.

Cal glanced over the paperwork. Then, he looked up and said, "Walker was born in England?"

"Yep, he and his mother lived in a flat in London. No mention of his father."

"Where's his mother now?"

"Says she died in '99, somewhere overseas," Andy said. "The report is vague as to where she died. Does that really matter?"

Cal thought for a moment, then shook his head.

"Keep reading."

Cal glanced through another sheet under the bio page. He quickly glanced up. "The guy was a sniper in the British Royal Marines!"

Andy smiled. "Yes, I thought you might like to know that."

Micco got up and scanned the report. "I wonder who his dad was."

Andy's cellphone rang, so he walked toward the kitchen area to answer it.

Just then, a 'Beep' came from the printer.

"Good," Micco said as he grabbed the paper and handed it to Cal. "You both are going to want to see this."

Andy joined them and asked, "What's this?" He looked over Cal's shoulder.

Micco said, "I was checking further into Luther's military records and found an attack his team handled in Iraq." Micco stopped for a moment, then added, "It was also in '99, he was a member of a Joint Special Operations Command – Delta Force."

"Jesus," Cal said. "I had no idea he was involved in this type of operation."

"Luther had a three-man team. I found one of his men, a Brian Lemke, who lived in San Francisco, but he died in a hit and run accident in 2009."

"That's interesting," Andy said.

Cal scanned the document, then compared the dates to Andy's file. He said, "Earlier to that hit and run accident in 2009, Ray Walker was discharged from the British military – he was caught going over secured records."

Micco glanced at his friend and said, "With Luther gone now, there's only one man left of his team still standing."

"Who's that?" Andy asked.

"Kyle Bevan—"

"Damn!" Cal said. "I met him when I went to Klamath Falls."

Andy looked at Cal. "That call was from Sheriff Morrow. We had a report that the tires on Walker's SUV matched our castings. So, I asked the sheriff to put out an ATL on his vehicle. It was spotted on Route 97 heading south."

Cal looked quickly between the two men and said, "I'll fly!"

ONCE THEY WERE IN the plane and took off, Andy said from a seat in the back, "I'd better call my boss to let him know what we're up to." He looked at the other men in the aircraft and added, "You know he's not going to like this."

"But," Cal said from the cockpit, "if we can save a man's life, I don't care who likes it."

Over the phone, Andy advised the sheriff of their position, asking to have the Klamath Falls authorities alerted.

Cal handed his phone to Micco. "Call Amanda and ask her to find her friend, Kyle! Her number's in my contacts."

While Micco made the call, Cal told Andy, "I knew there was something about this guy that bothered me. I didn't get it until now. When we were at Holt Construction, he signed a delivery order – he used his left hand. The ME said the assailant was probably left handed."

Andy nodded excitedly. "Walker also worked with Holt for two years – started just before that fire at Hawk Plastics."

Over the Cessna's engine, Cal yelled, "Okay, that's way too many coincidences for my taste!"

CHAPTER 46

WHEN THEY LANDED AT the Klamath Regional Airport, they were met by Hal Jewett, the local sheriff, and a couple of deputies. Andy began to fill the officials in.

"Sheriff Jewett, I'm Detective Shaw with the Deschutes County Sheriff's Office. We have a suspicion that one of our murder suspects is here in Klamath Falls. Our ATL was issued for his vehicle."

Andy turned to Cal and Micco and introduced them. "These two are our...uh, consultants on this case."

Jewett said to Andy, "Sherriff Morrow called to say he's on his way. But, I thought this case was closed."

"We have new evidence to prove otherwise," Andy responded.

The sheriff smiled and added, "I'm glad Morrow said he was leaving Rupert behind."

Andy nodded and asked where the perpetrator was now.

"We lost site of the vehicle after it arrived in the city limits," one of the deputies said.

"Damn it!" Andy said. "I'm afraid a man's life is at stake here."

Just then, Cal's phone rang. He rolled his eyes at Micco as the bagpipe song played, so he stepped away from the group. When Cal saw Amanda's name on the screen, he quickly answered the call.

"Kyle is here," Amanda's voice said.

"Keep him there," Cal said. "We're on our way."

"What's going on?" she asked anxiously.

"I'll explain later. Just don't let Kyle leave."

When he hung up, he returned to the others and said, "I know where Walker is."

As they walked toward one of the squad cars, Andy leaned in and said softly to Cal, "I'm glad you're here. I have a feeling we're going to need your kind of backup."

"No sirens," Cal cautioned.

Everyone got into the vehicles and left the airport.

CHAPTER 47

WITH SIRENS AND LIGHTS off, the two local squad cars approached the road to Amanda's house.

"The owner of our ATL vehicle is Ray Walker – he's a trained sniper," Andy cautioned.

"We think his target is a man named Kyle Bevan," Cal informed the sheriff. "He's a UPS driver here."

"Now, why would a UPS driver be a murder victim?" the deputy driving the car asked.

Cal didn't answer.

Andy stepped in and said, "We've been tracking Walker for some time now. Bevan was a team member in the military with our murder victim."

"There's the vehicle," Andy said when he saw a black Land Rover parked along the side of the road. He cautioned the KFSO deputy to park a block away.

In the distance, it was quiet at Amanda's house. Too quiet for Cal's liking. He could see Kyle's UPS truck in the driveway, but there was no movement. A quick flash of light caught his eye and he looked at Micco. Without a word, his friend nodded.

"Give us a minute," Cal said softly to Andy. Then, he and Micco got out first, leaving the car door open to avoid any noise.

"Where the hell is he going?" the local sheriff asked.

"Cal's checking around the back—"

"I don't want some rogue cowboy messing this operation up," Jewett hissed.

"He's no cowboy," Andy said. "He's a Marine Special Ops Commander. We can cover the front of the house from here."

AS CAL AND MICCO quietly went to the back of a nearby house, he signaled Micco to take a wide sweep around the other way.

Crouched down under a large evergreen, Cal waited. This wasn't a war zone, but he went into action as if he were in one.

First he saw a small movement in the bushes, then the glint of light again. Cal slowly crept closer and finally made out the shadow of a man in position - a rifle with a scope and suppressor aimed at Amanda's large front window. When he saw Andy and the sheriff's men approaching the front door, Cal knew he had to move fast.

Just as the local deputy was escorting Kyle from the house, Cal attacked.

The man in camo gear and a ski mask reacted quickly. He dropped the rifle and knocked Cal to the ground. The two men fought, then the man reach for a knife in a sheath tied to the outside of his left leg. Cal knew a knife was much more dangerous than a gun.

Circling to cause the man to focus on his position, Cal gauged the angle of the knife - which was pointed right at his chest. He used a move he'd been taught in Taekwondo, using both of his hands to knock the knife from the man's hand.

Micco came flying out of the woods and took the man to the ground, pinning him under his body.

Cal knew who the man was before the mask was removed. "Ray Walker," Cal said as he used his handkerchief to pick up the knife and saw the broken tip.

Just then, Andy and two of the sheriff's men arrived and Walker was arrested.

Cal was fuming as the deputies led Walker toward a squad car. "Those idiots should not have brought Kyle out - they just made him an easier target."

"I don't think they understood the severity of the situation," Andy said, trying to cover for his fellow officers.

Taking a deep breath, Cal said, "You're probably right." He leaned in to his friend and said, "Here's Walker's knife. It's an F-S fighting knife. They were used in the U.K. military - and it's missing a point."

With a gloved hand, Andy also picked up the rifle and smiled. "If this rifle matches the bullet that shot the cougar, we got our man."

One of the local deputies came up and took the knife and rifle. "I've got these," he said.

Andy looked at his two friends. "Thanks for all your help."

Cal nodded. "You might want to come inside."

MICCO WAITED OUTSIDE WITH one of the deputies while Cal and Andy went up to Amanda's house to let them know Kyle was safe.

"Who the hell was that?" Kyle asked as he watched the

man in handcuffs being escorted to a sheriff's squad car.

"Ray Walker – a man who wanted to kill you," Andy said.

"Why?" Kyle asked, then his face went white. "Wait - did you say Walker?"

"Yes."

Kyle was quiet for a moment and looked over at Amanda. Then he said, "My last mission with Luther has haunted me for years. Our team went into enemy territory and determined the coordinates where our missiles were to be fired. The intel was that a terrorist cell was working out of a small village outside of Baghdad. After we sent the order for the rockets, we hightailed it out of there. Afterwards, we learned that one U.K. civilian was among the dead. Her name was Walker."

"You did what you were ordered to do," Cal said.

He looked over and saw that Amanda was now understanding why Kyle never talked about his job in the military.

Kyle only nodded.

"You're the last man alive on your team," Cal said.

Sighing heavily, Kyle said, "I know. But, I had no idea we were being targeted. Brian's death was a car accident – or so I thought. And, now I know Luther's is connected."

"You're safe now," Andy said. "But, you'll need to go to the sheriff's office to give a statement."

Cal said, "I've got to get back home."

Kyle shook both men's hands. "You saved my life. Thank you!"

Amanda said to Cal, "I never believed Bobby could kill Luther."

CHAPTER 48

RAY WALKER SAT HANDCUFFED across from Sheriff Scott Morrow in the Klamath County Sheriff's Office interrogation room. Ray kept looking at the mirror, which made Andy a little nervous.

"I sometimes wonder if they can see us behind these two-way mirrors," Andy said as he, Cal and Micco stood on the other side.

"He just assumes someone is watching," Cal assured him. "I'm glad I had Micco give Morrow his report on Luther's military background."

Sheriff Jewett came in and joined them. "I thought since our charge is only Attempted Murder, I'd let Scott do the questioning."

They all watched as the red light on the video camera blinked in the corner of the room. Morrow opened the file on the table. "You were born in England, is that correct?"

Walker nodded.

"I see that you had U. K. military training."

Walker moved in his seat, but didn't say anything.

"Why did you kill Luther Greeves and attempt to kill Kyle Bevan?"

When Morrow didn't get a response, he slammed his fist on the table. "Damn it, we have evidence to tie you to Greeves' murder and you were caught red-handed here in Klamath Falls about to shoot Bevan. What was your motive for killing these men?"

Walker looked gravely at the sheriff. "They killed my parents."

Morrow sat speechless. This was the last response he expected.

"But I thought your parents lived in England."

Leaning his elbows onto the table, Walker moved in closer to the man across from him.

"My mother was English...Later, I learned that my father was Arabic. Luther Greeves' unit was responsible for the attack on my father's home in Baghdad..." He looked at the mirror and smiled. "I'm just sorry I failed to get the last man on Greeves' team."

Morrow looked through some papers in the file and asked, "For the record, does that mean that you are admitting to killing Luther Greeves and attempting to kill Kyle Bevin?"

Walker smiled. "Yes, and I ran the other one down while he was jogging."

Behind the glass, Andy said, "Well, that was easy."

"Scott is good at his job," Jewett said.

Andy smiled and said, "Yes he is."

"Walker's been waiting a long time for this," Cal said. He'd seen cases involving vengeance and knew how that type of hatred could drive a person to do almost anything. He'd even felt it himself.

A few seconds passed before Morrow continued his interrogation. "How did you know about the men who worked with Luther?"

"In Surrey, I worked in the Administration office before going into sniper training. That's how I learned about my father and what village he lived in."

Walker looked down at the floor for a long moment, then added, "I didn't know my mother was there with him at the time the U.S. artillery sent in their bombs. When my office heard the news, I looked up everything I could find about that attack…that's when I went into sniper training."

Looking again at the glass, Walker added, "I want the world to know what these men did to my family."

AS WALKER WAS BEING charged, Cal and Micco stood talking with Andy in the bullpen.

"That guy also confessed to setting the fire at Hawk Plastics last year," Andy said as he laid the file on a desk. "He's going to be in prison for a long time."

Cal thought for a moment, then said, "After being in the Middle East, I can understand why some people snap like that – wanting to settle a score after losing people close to them. That doesn't justify what he did, but war is never fair."

As the two sheriffs walked out of the holding cell area, Jewett said to Morrow, "We make a great team."

"Hal," Morrow said, "we always did. I haven't seen you in about a year. Got time for a coffee?"

"Sure," Jewett said, grabbing his hat. "I'll be outside."

Morrow turned to Andy. "Help finish processing Walker, okay? We'll take him back to Bend later."

"I'm on it, Chief," Andy answered with a salute.

"You did good today," Morrow said to his deputy, "even if you went off book."

Cal and Micco were about to leave when Morrow slapped Cal on the back and said, "You were a great help on this case, son. And your sidekick, too."

Cal thanked him and saw Micco wince. He knew his buddy hated being a sidekick to anyone.

"We could use men like you in Bend."

"Well, Sheriff," Cal said, "I don't know about Micco, but I'm still on government duty."

CHAPTER 49

CAL WAS THANKFUL WHEN he finally set the Cessna down on the grass landing strip at the Double J. It had been a long couple of weeks.

Before they left the Klamath Falls Sheriff's Office, Cal had called Amanda to tell her about Walker's confession so she could let Kyle know he was no longer in any danger.

As he taxied the plane to the hangar, he rolled his shoulder to ease the stiffness that had settled in.

"You okay?" Micco asked in the seat next to him.

"Yeah, just tired."

"That wasn't the first time I had to save your butt," Micco said smiling.

"You know I was steering Walker so you could jump him," Cal said.

The two men sat silently in the plane's cockpit for a while. Cal thought of how there had been no time to grieve the loss of his friend, Luther. On some of his missions, there was never enough time.

"I'm just glad that's over," Cal sighed, looking at Mt. Bachelor on the horizon.

"Me, too." Micco looked at his friend and waited.

"What?"

Micco didn't say anything.

Eventually, Cal knew his friend could read his mind and opened up. "I talked with Major Gray a couple of days ago."

Micco only waited.

"I've got my twenty years in now...maybe it's time..."

"You'll like retirement," Micco finally said, smiling. "I know I do."

Cal turned and looked at his friend. "But, what will I do?"

"That's the beauty of it – anything you want."

Cal smiled and the two men got out of the plane.

WHEN THEY WALKED FROM the hangar, Glenn came out to meet them.

"I heard what you two have been up to," he said. "You did a good thing today." Glenn hugged Cal and added, "I'm so proud of you."

Just then, Mary drove in with Jamie's kids.

"What're you doing here?" Cal asked as he held the door open for Mary.

"I have a surprise for Winnie," she said, then went around and opened the trunk of her car. She took out a square, brown-paper wrapped parcel.

"She's in the house," Glenn said. Then, he asked the kids, "Would you like to go see the horses?"

Excitedly, Riley and Josie agreed and the three-some went toward the stable.

"I've got some work to finish up," Micco said and left.

When he was alone with Mary, Cal said, "We got the guy. It was a man out for vengeance. But, we finally have some closure for Jamie."

"Who was it?"

"A guy who knew Luther. I can't really say much more than that."

"I'll let Jamie know. She'll be glad to put all of this behind them."

AS THEY ENTERED THE house, Winnie came out of the kitchen, wiping her hands on a dishtowel.

"Hello, Mary. We've just had our lunch. Have you eaten?"

"Yes, thank you."

"Cal? Can I get you anything?"

"I'm good."

He went and sat down in an armchair in the living room. His body still ached from the tension, his shoulder now pulsating.

Mary handed the parcel to Winnie. "This is for you – a thank you for all you taught me."

"Oh my, you needn't have done this."

"I know. But, you are such an inspiration."

Winnie took the parcel to the long table behind the couch and began to unwrap it. "Oh, my," she sighed as she gazed at the canvas. Tears came to her eyes and Cal walked over to see what it was.

The soft colors of the Crooked River landscape seemed to come to life with the tiny stones, pine cones and grasses near the water's edge. She had captured the canyon beautifully. He looked at a figure in the foreground and realized she had painted a small image of Winnie, gathering rocks as she loved to do.

"I used the agate I found to get my red pigment, like you showed me," Mary said. "The grass and small pine cones came from a field behind Jamie's house."

"It's beautiful!" Winnie said and hugged her new friend. "It seems the pupil has surpassed me. Thank you, I will treasure it always."

Glenn came in with the kids.

"Aunt Mary," Riley said excitedly, "I'm going to adopt a mustang."

"We'll have to see what your mom thinks, first," Mary cautioned him.

"I got to pet a cow," Josie said, giggling. "It looked like an Oreo cookie, with white stuffing inside."

"That was probably 'Cookie Monster'," Winnie added. "She's my favorite and she always looks to see if I have a treat in my pocket."

"Galloway cattle are so docile," Glenn said. "Each has their own personality – they're just like children."

"Okay, kids," Mary said. "Time to go."

"We'll be saying goodbye," Glenn said, placing his arm around his wife. "Come back anytime."

CAL WALKED OUT WITH Mary. The kids ran and got into the car. But, Mary went to the trunk and opened it.

She came back to where Cal stood and gave him a painting. As she handed it to him, she said, "This is for you."

The image was striking. Bravo, Cal's mustang, stood with the mountains in the background. The horse's mane and tail seemed to be blown by an imaginary wind. It was Cal's favorite view on the Double J.

"Thank you," he said. "This is amazing!"

"No, thank you!" Mary leaned over and gave him a kiss on the cheek.

Before opening her door, Cal asked, "When are you going back to Seattle?"

"I haven't decided."

CHAPTER 50

AFTER MARY LEFT, CAL went up to Micco's room, carrying the painting.

"What's that?" his friend asked from the couch.

"Something Mary did for me."

He set the painting on the counter and leaned it against the wall.

"I think she caught your essence," Micco said, smiling.

Cal went to the fridge and pulled out two bottles of beer. After popping the caps, he took one to Micco.

Plopping down next to his friend, they each took a long swig of the cold brew.

"Ah," Cal sighed. "This hits the spot."

"A job well done, my friend," Micco said.

"Cheers," Cal said and the two clinked their bottles together.

They sat silently for some time. It was one of their rituals they'd done since their first beer, after they finished whatever chore Cal's dad had assigned them on the ranch.

Cal thoughts shifted to his dad and he took another sip.

After a while, Micco said, "Have you made your decision yet?"

"I haven't had time—"

"Come on, I know you've been vacillating about this for quite a while now."

Cal finally nodded. "I saw how tired Glenn looked after he came back with the kids today. I need to be here."

"Oorah!" Micco said, clinking his bottle against Cal's again.

"Now what? So, I become a rancher?" Cal asked.

Micco grinned. "I think we can come up with more than just ranch work."

Cal looked at his friend. He always knew when Micco was up to something.

"You should become a P.I.," Micco said. "And, I can be your tech support."

"Why would I want to do that?"

"So we can do what we just did – chasing bad guys and helping people find closure. We've always made a good team."

Cal looked out a window. "That's not exactly what I had in mind. I'll have to think about it."

"Don't take too long. Your leave is about up."

"Yeah, I know. By the way, Andy told me he's looking into going over to the State Police Department as a detective."

Micco nodded. "That could be very helpful for a Private Investigator."

They sat in silence for some time.

Finally, Cal slapped his hands on his knees and got up. "If we're going to do this," he said as he tossed Micco his cellphone, "change my damned ringtone back!"

THE END

ABOUT THE AUTHOR

This is Linda Kuhlmann's fifth novel – the first in the Cal Jamison Mystery Series. Prior to this book, she wrote the *Koenig Triple Crown Series,* which began with a family mystery that evolved into a fictional portrayal of the horseracing underworld. She has also written an unrelated novel, *The Red Boots,* set in both Ireland and Oregon, and a small non-fiction booklet for Kindle called *Shameless Marketing for Writers.* Ms. Kuhlmann lives in Oregon.

Made in the USA
Las Vegas, NV
16 December 2022

62817953R10129